HER GREAT ESCAPE

(THE FINAL CHAPTER)

SHANTANEL PAYNE

Printed in the United States of America
ISBN: 979-8-218-78450-8
First Printing, 2025
Shreveport, LA 71119

PROLOGUE

In the blink of an eye, her world transformed into a fierce storm of emotions. The intoxicating scent of him clung to her like a warm embrace, his smooth skin felt like silk against her fingertips, and the surge of dopamine from the smell of his soft, curly hair filled her nostrils, igniting an emotional bond deeper than words could ever express, one that only a mother could truly comprehend.

The RV ride was rough for Summer. It felt like David hit every bump on the highway, causing the large trailer to shake violently. The pressure in her lower abdomen felt intense, as if her entire uterus might fall out. Her stitches from the cesarean section pulled taut and stung with the slightest of movement.

Asher consumed her chest, snuggled tightly like a little bundle of joy, radiating warmth and a profound sense of contentment. Occasionally, his soft, sweet lip-smacking would stir her from her drowsiness as his tiny head lifted slightly in search of his next meal. Her swollen, throbbing breast seemed to be in sync with his feedings, creating a moment of tenderness and connection.

Summer found herself unable to move, wedged between Rose and Stevin, both of whom refused to leave her side. She didn't mind their close presence: their closeness provided a comforting shield against the relentless shadows of her nightmares; that haunted her thoughts, leaving her trembling, and struggling to distinguish between the chilling horror of her dreams and reality. Having barely managed to escape two prisons, she knew her hell was far from over. Christopher would be lurking, poised to strike at the most unsuspecting moment, ready to plunge her back into darkness.

CHAPTER: 1
WHERE'S MY DAUGHTER

The clock ticked loudly, serving as a throbbing reminder of why she was there. The room smelled of fresh paint fumes, and the four white walls were bare as the room seemed to shrink in size with each passing minute.

A blush of sunlight peeped in through the broken blinds that were covered in cobwebs. The ample fluorescent light hung from the ceiling, and the bright LED light blinded Rose's sensitive eyes, which had not rested in three days.

Rose was a nervous wreck; she had broken every promise she had made to Stevin and Summer. Her cuticles were absent and ragged from biting her nails from the overwhelming stress and anxiety she had been under.

Running her teeth across her nail beds, she had gnawed them down to raw, nerve-exposed stumps, causing numbness and tingling in her fingers.

This distracted her while she nervously paced the floor and then returned to her chair. She snatched up her phone several times and slammed it back down on the table, a surge of frustration washing over her when she noticed no missed calls or texts updating her with any news. She needed David by her side. Afraid to face this alone, she felt she had no choice. She was willing to walk to the end of the earth alone if necessary.

A slight tap on the door jolted her from her deep thoughts. As the detectives entered the room and approached her, one with his head hung low, shoulder slumped, his body language screaming bad news. Rose jumped up from the chair before the detectives could speak, assuming the worst, as she screamed and cried out, "WHERE IS MY DAUGHTER?"

Stephanie stepped off the unit to place a personal call to Dr. Brown.

"Hello, sir; I was standing at the nurse's station when administration called down looking for Dr. Santos. They had paged him a couple of times overhead when the phone rang at the nurse's station. I hurried and picked up, but he asked for Sandra. I stood over her, reading the orders as she was writing.

"Sir, I'm pretty sure it's Summer. He has requested a private room and ordered the attending nurse to be Sandra. Here's the kicker: the patient is being checked in under Jane Doe."

"Listen, Stephanie, we can't screw this up. I will never forget her mom's face when she arrived, and I had to inform her I no longer knew her daughter's whereabouts. The moment that patient arrives, you page me. If it's indeed Summer, you immediately notify her mom. I want her family flown out on the next plane available, even if I have to pay for it."

"Dr. Santos is currently stuck in rush hour traffic, sir. He requested that Dr. DeKosky attend to this particular patient if she arrived before him. Room 1406 needs an amniotomy completed. This is also one of Dr. Santos's high-risk patients whose carrying twins in separate sacks. I will get Dr. DeKosky on this now and tie him up with this patient."

"Great, Stephanie, I don't want to make any moves until we are sure it's her. We will not fail her this time, and that is a promise!"

Chapter: 2
The Big Mission

Atlanta Georgia

Rose's attention was suddenly captured as she stared at her cell phone. The screen showed an incoming call from Stephanie, the nurse at Los Angeles Health Medical Center who had cared for Summer upon her return to the States. Rose's body jolted upright in bed, startling David, who she clutched onto tightly. Her hand shook, and her eyes widened, brimming with tears. David urgently urged her to put the call on speaker, but his words were a distant murmur as Rose was completely engrossed in the conversation, and nothing could break her concentration.

"Rose, Stephanie shouted, "We got her! Rose, she's back at LAH."

"Stephanie, please tell me my daughter is okay?"

"She's stable, Rose. I won't lie to you. She is in active labor. She arrived with the baby in distress, and Summer herself arrived with a potentially dangerous complication. She is suffering from severe pre-eclampsia, which warrants an immediate cesarean.

"She is being prepped as we speak. I must hang up now. Dr. Brown is doing the delivery and requested you guys fly out tonight. And Rose, it's vitally important for you guys to call me personally. Do not attempt to call and ask for Summer. The only way we can assist you in getting your daughter back is to follow the instructions I or Dr. Brown will text. Our window is crucial; we have no room for error. Try not to stress, Rose; Dr. Brown is an excellent doctor."

"David, she's back at the hospital. She's in labor, but they have to take the baby by cesarean," Rose cried out. "We must go now, David... Right now!"

"Calm down, Rose, and breathe. You start packing, and I need to make some calls to get myself covered with my patients."

Rose frantically threw clothes in the luggage while David could be heard canceling his patients appointments, requesting for another psych doctor to be reassigned to his patients, as he had a family emergency and needed to leave town immediately.

"David, hurry and get dressed," Rose urgently urged him. "We will call Stevin from the car. I will take the luggage out and place it in the car."

"Woman, don't you dare touch that suitcase; I will carry it down on my way out," David said as he approached her, rubbing her shoulders. "Rose, calm down. I've got a good feeling about this," he added before stepping away with a disheartening look. "But I don't think getting Stevin involved just yet is a great idea."

"No, David!"

"Stevin would never forgive us if we withheld this from him. He has every right to know and be there, and besides, he's the child's father."

"I know, Rose. It's just that Stevin has found comfort in the bottle since Summer's disappearance, being forced to take a leave from work and moving back home with his parents. He's just not himself. I counsel him as much as possible, but he's drunk on most of our calls. What if he shows up and can't control his emotions? Besides, we are not 100% certain if Stevin is the father. Then what? We can't risk it, Rose."

"David, I wholeheartedly believe Stevin will show up and be the partner and father we have grown to love. Let's give him a chance. He's suffering, David. He blames himself," Rose said as she burst into tears, her face burying into David's bare chest. "He is the father, David; he just has to be!"

"Calm down, sweetheart; I will personally take responsibility for our son in California."

Rose looked up at David with her tear-streaked face, her eyes filled with a mix of hope and fear. The corner of her mouth curved slightly, attempting a smile. David's statement sent a surge of hope through her. 'That's correct, our son,' she thought, her heart swelling with anticipation. Finally, her family would be together again.

"David, let's also reach out to Kimberley. We might need her to assist us. Go ahead and finish getting dressed; I will be down in the car booking our flights. Let's just pray we can book something immediately," she said, her voice trembling with anxiety, worrying that a flight wouldn't be available in time.

Rose was relieved when she was able to book all three tickets for a flight departing within the hour. She had notified Kimberley, who immediately took a ride share to the airport without question. Anxiously sitting in the car, Rose watched as David took his time exiting the home, finally locking up when she noticed he had packed more luggage.

"David, what are you doing? We need to get to the airport now!" Rose exclaimed.

"Rose, I watched you pack; you never touched the underwear drawer. I had to ensure we had the necessary essentials for this trip."

"David, did you reach out to Stevin? Kimberley is on her way to the airport now."

"No, let me call him now. By the way, how was that conversation with Kimberley?" David inquired.

"Honestly, she asked where she needed to be and what time. She released the line, saying she would meet us there. No questions asked."

"Rose, it's time for us to cut her some slack. She's trying."

"I know David, and I'm trying as well."

"I know you are, sweetheart," he said, rubbing her leg.

King County, Washington

Stevin quickly answered when he noticed David's number displayed on the screen.

"Hello, David," Stevin said in a curious voice. He stopped allowing himself to be hopeful months ago.

"Stevin, I need you to listen carefully and follow my instructions. Get to the airport; Summer is back in the hospital," David urgently instructed. "Hello... Hello," David repeated as Stevin released the line.

"Dammit, Rose, this is what I was afraid of." David tried calling him back without success. When Stevin finally returned his call.

"Son, you have to listen. We can't help her if we are all not on the same page."

"I understand David, I'm sorry. I needed to book my flight. I will call you on my way to the airport; I must make it on time to catch the flight I just booked. I will make it before you guys. I will get instructions when I phone you back," Stevin said as the call abruptly ended again.

David was too distracted to attempt to call him back by Rose climbing the seat after receiving a text. She burst into excited tears as she stared at a photo of her grandchild.

"Oh, David, he is so beautiful," she said as she frantically dialed Stevin's number. "I must hear Stevin's reaction when he sees him for the first time. He's his twin.

"Hello, Mom, I can't talk. I'm about to miss the flight I booked if I'm not out the door soon," Stevin said, attempting to rush Rose off the line.

"Son, look at the message I just sent you."

"Okay, Mom, I will once I'm in the car."

"No, son! I need you to look now," Rose said authoritatively.

All could be heard was Stevin sobbing on the other end as Mr. Bash Sr. comforted him, encouraging him, while Rose held the phone, sobbing.

Stephanie had sent a picture of the baby looking healthy and sucking on his tiny fingers. Alone with a text instructing Rose what to do.

"*Rose, the baby is healthy. Summer is stable, but she did lose a large amount of blood and is having to be transfused. Do not worry; her vitals are stable. My shift is ending now. We have a hotel across the street from the hospital; I will book the room, and Dr. Brown will cover the costs. I will text you guys the information. Please meet with me first. My boyfriend works security; luckily for us, the 4th-floor security cameras are down. Dr. Brown is keeping Summer in the labor unit, so the bodyguards are not allowed. Dr. Santos has left the hospital for the day. Will keep you updated.*"

CHAPTER: 3
RESCUING SUMMER

Mr. Bash Sr. hurried to Stevin's side, his heart-wrenching at the sight of his son sobbing, slumped over, pressing his cell phone to his chest. Stevin, his hands trembling, pressed his cell phone into his father's hand, a silent plea for comfort in a moment only a father could understand.

Mr. Bash's gaze flickered over Stevin's phone, then he stepped away, disappearing into the depths of their home. He returned, holding a faded photograph of Stevin as a newborn, the edges worn from years of fond memories.

"He's yours, son, without a shadow of a doubt." Mr. Bash said, his voice filled with conviction. "He is a mirror image of you, a true testament to our shared traits."

Mr. Bash dropped to his knees, his arms wrapping around Stevin in a tight embrace that seemed to shake Stevin's emotional state. Stevin, at thirty-five, was witnessing a sight he had never seen before - his father, his pillar of strength, shedding tears.

"Now rise to your feet," Mr. Bash spoke in his military demeanor. "I need you to get your head in the game, son, and bring my grandson home." Turning back to Stevin, he said, "And son this is not a mission that needs to be led with emotions."

"Thanks, pop. I need one favor that only you and your connections can pull off."

"And what is that son?"

"I need to know where Christopher is being treated. Rose stated she was informed that Summer and her husband had been injured. But Christopher was never registered as a patient. My thoughts are that his father had him locked back up in the nut house. I need his location and some credentials to get in and see him."

"I'm confident I can handle that; I won't ask why, but I trust you understand the gravity of the situation. I'm pretty sure I have an idea why. There's no closure like staring down your defeated enemy in their eyes after you have won the battle. Just ensure it's not at Summer's expense. Now head on out before you miss your flight; check your email; I will get that information to you."

Stevin exited the home, requesting Mr. Bash only share the news with Mrs. Irene after he had gone. Stevin's mom was no longer a fan of Summer after learning about her situation and watching her once confident son being reduced to a mere shell of himself, using alcohol to cope. He and his father failed to mention the baby until they were certain they could locate Summer. It was another blow to the heart that Stevin refused to subject his mom to.

As he sped down the freeway, he prayed he wouldn't get pulled over; he had no time to spare. He had arranged for his cousin Ciara and her husband to meet him at the airport so he wouldn't have to wait to find parking. He barely made the gate and had to persuade the flight attendant to reopen the door and allow him on the flight, garnishing stares from onlookers.

Settling into his seat, he stared at his son's picture and worried about Summer's health. Rose had informed him Summer had been moved to the ICU for better monitoring after having a reaction to a blood transfusion.

Stevin was ordered to stay away from the hospital; he was provided with Stephanie's contact information to reach out once he arrived. The only thing that comforted him was that Summer was in a location where she could be monitored and receive proper care, and not one of Mr. Diamond's goons could get to her. He was willing to play by their rules, but only for a short time.

Hartsfield-Jackson Atlanta International Airport

With her heart pounding, Kimberley arrived at the airport before her parents. She stood in the baggage check-in area on her arrival, filled with a mix of hope and anxiety about their impending reunion.

As she spotted them approaching, she couldn't help but feel a surge of nervousness overcome her, her mind racing with uncertainty, unsure of how she would be received.

David's arms wrapped around her with a welcoming smile, grabbing her around the neck and fully embracing her with a hug. Rose reached over, only offering a light pat on the back, a gesture that felt more like she were an unwelcome guest.

Kimberley attempted to hide her broken heart as she fought to hold back her tears. Sensing her struggle, David pulled her closer, assuring her everything would be okay.

"Give her time, baby girl. I truly believe that if we can get your sister home, all will be forgiven."

Los Angeles, California

Stevin followed all instructions as given. He arrived at the airport, rented a car, and contacted Stephanie on her burner phone as instructed. When he arrived at the hotel, he was surprised by Stephanie's warm, bubbly embrace as she jumped into his arms, her excitement evident.

"Excuse me; I'm just so excited for you guys, " she said. "Let's take you upstairs and drop your bags off. I can't wait until you see your son," she said.

Stevin eyes widen with surprise. He had assumed they would attempt to keep him away. "Are you saying I will get to see them?" He asked.

"I can't risk you seeing Summer; there are cameras everywhere on that unit. The cameras are down on the 4th floor due to some AI updates in the system that the IT department is behind on. I will walk you over and scan you in using the back entrance stairway.

"First, I need you to change into these scrubs; we have several cesarean schedule tonight. You will blend right in. You must keep your hat and facemask on at all times. Summer's father-in-law..."

Stephanie quickly rephrased her statement, seeing Stevin's facial reaction.

"I mean, Mr. Diamond's hired men seem to have been called off since Summer is in the ICU. But that doesn't mean they're not lurking. I made you a bracelet. Show this at the window, and they will place the baby closer to the show window in the nursery.

"Stevin, please don't try anything; I promise we have a plan to assist Summer. She is actually stable enough to be placed back on the floor. The only reason why she hasn't been moved is because she hasn't awoken."

Stevin's eyes widened. "Don't worry, Stevin; her body is exhausted. We will never know what she endured. She's a fighter; most people her size, with the number of injuries she suffered, would be dead. All her vitals are stable. She needs the rest; besides, it gives us the opportunity to break her free from that psycho family.

***

Stephanie walked ahead to the hospital while Stevin followed behind, keeping a couple of feet distance as if they weren't together.

"Stevin, this is as far as I can go. I can't risk being seen with you. I have been off the clock for five hours now. I couldn't explain why I was back on the unit. Tell Rose I will stop by before I start my morning shift, and I will schedule a time for them to visit tomorrow. Be careful; remember, if anyone else comes to the window, walk away.

"Just hook a right, and the nursery is located on the left-hand side," Stephanie said, directing Stevin.

Stevin cautiously approached the large window, his heart pounding in his chest. He scanned the cribs, his eyes darting from one crib to another, searching for the name tag labeled 'Diamond.' The mere thought of Summer and his son being connected to that name sent a cold shiver racing down his spine and made his stomach churn, causing bile to rise in his throat. As he looked around the nursery, a nurse walked over to close the blinds and gestured for him to pick up the phone located on the wall.

"I'm sorry, sir," she says, her voice tinged with urgency. "We have just changed shifts, and my coworker is running late. I am currently the only nursery nurse, and I must start my assessments, so at this time, the window will be closed."

Stevin, feeling defeated, knew not to make a big fuss. He simply dropped his head and returned the phone on the hook, silently accepting his current situation.

The nurse, Amy, immediately feels guilty and taps on the window, signaling him to pick up the phone.

"Which baby is yours?"

Stevin shrugs his shoulders as if he was saying, 'I don't know.'

Amy let out a light-hearted giggle. "Name, I am asking for the last name?"

"Diamond," Stevin replied.

Amy instantly knew he was referring to the infant whose mother was in the ICU.

"Are you dad?"

Stevin shook his head yes. Amy placed her hand over her heart with a silent plea of sorrow. "Do you have your bracelet?"

Stevin held up the bracelet he had received from Stephanie. Amy signaled for him to head to the nursery door.

She greeted Stevin at the door and was quite a chatterbox. "So, I got in report that your wife is doing better. I know you probably already know this about her condition. But that's great to hear she is doing well.

"Because of the circumstance of your wife's birthing complication, it robbed you guys of your bonding time with the baby. We like to call it the golden hour. So, let's get you set up. I just need you to sign in with your identification."

Stevin's smile quickly faded. "Oh... I need to run out to my car. I placed my wallet in my wife's purse and locked everything in the trunk."

Amy paused momentarily, as if she would reinforce the policies, then turned to him saying, "You've been through enough today, come on."

She led Stevin to a private room located inside the nursery and instructed him to sit in the rocking chair and remove his shirt. "I will go collect your little bundle of joy."

Stevin's heart raced with anticipation as he prepared to meet his son for the first time. He could hear the wheels of the bassinet being pushed into the room as he held his breath, feeling like something was about to happen and snatch this moment away from him.

"Here we go," Amy said as she unwrapped the baby from the blankets and placed him skin-to-skin on Stevin's chest. She also placed a warm blanket over Stevin.

He took a deep breath and sobbed as his tears collected in his son's hair. He attempted to pinch his tear ducks and stop the waterworks, but his emotions were high. He couldn't explain what he was feeling at that very moment.

Wiggling his phone out the back pocket of the scrub pants he was wearing, he took multiple photos before video calling his dad. When Mr. Bash Sr. answered, his mom was also visible on the screen, as they both refused to turn in until they knew he was safe and had called with an update.

Stevin's face was all they could see when he held his pointer finger to his lips, signaling for them to be quiet. He muted the volume before easing the baby into his arms and turning the camera on the baby.

Mrs. Irene jumped for joy as she grabbed hold of her husband and cried tears of relief. After Stevin left for the airport Mr. Bash showed her the photo of the baby Stevin received, and without a doubt, he was a Bash baby.

Stevin texted, "*I love you guys. I will reach out in the morning. Please get some rest.*"

Placing the baby back on his chest, he sat and rocked him for a few more minutes when he heard the second nurse arrive for her shift. Pulling the paper scrub cap down to his eyes, he placed his mask back on and waited for Amy to return.

"Hey, Dad, we need to start taking the babies to the rooms. I will give you another five minutes."

"I understand; you can take him," Stevin replied.

Before Amy could swaddle the baby back into his blanket, Stevin had slipped out the door, racing to the stairwell. He reached the room, closed the door, placed his back against it, and slid to the floor. Overwhelmed with emotions, he stared at his son's photos. This would be his secret, a sacred moment he chose to keep to himself. He decided not to share his bonding experience with his son with Rose and Stephanie. He wanted to ensure that no one spoils his first moments with his son.

Chapter: 4
The Betrayal

The ringing of his cell phone awakened Stevin. Rose and David had arrived and needed access to the suite. He dragged himself out of bed and greeted them at the door. To his surprise, Kimberley strolled in last, pulling her suitcase. He immediately released the door, causing it to swing back against her arm. Kimberley pushed the door back open with force. This angered her, but she had to accept Stevin's frustration towards her; it was her actions that had indirectly led to Christopher finding and kidnapping Summer, and she couldn't help but blame herself.

Stevin walked off, closing his bedroom door with force; this angered him. 'What were Rose and David thinking bringing her here,' he thought.

It was only a two-bedroom suite, and he certainly wasn't giving up his bed for that dizzy bitch.

"David, we should have given Stevin a heads up that we were bringing Kimberley with us," Rose said, sounding worried.

"Rose, she's trying her best, and it's time you and Stevin give her a chance. She's owning her mistakes and has been trying to help find Summer on her own. I will talk to Stevin tomorrow, but I will not turn my back on my daughter."

David exited their bedroom and located Kimberley sitting at the table crying. "Come here, baby girl; Dad will fix this for you."

"Thanks, Dad, but only I can fix what I have broken."

"Well, let me call the front desk and get you a rollaway bed."

"No, Dad, I'm okay with the couch. I've been traveling back and forth between my apartment in Atlanta and Minnesota. I've gotten used to sleeping in uncomfortable environments."

"Okay, hun, Dad will see you in the morning," David said as he kissed her forehead and returned to the bedroom.

What was clearly noticeable is that Rose never came out to say goodnight.

***

The ringing of Rose's phone awakened David and Rose.

"Hello," Rose answered with sleep still in her voice.

"Sorry for waking you, Rose."

"There's absolutely no reason for you to apologize, Stephanie. We got in about two hours ago. I am glad you woke me. Any news?"

"Yes, we will be transferring Summer back to the postpartum unit per Dr. Santos's orders. I have yet to see any of the men who were guarding her door. I need you guys to walk over. There are face masks at the entrance, so please wear one. Room 1400 has been blocked off for a patient Dr. Brown will be admitting at 11am. Come to that room and keep the door closed. I will bring the baby to the room for only a short moment. When we transfer Summer to the unit, I will also text you. When you receive the text, walk to the elevators and wait until we pass with her. I received in report that she is responding to physical stimuli but is still not fully awake. But she is doing well. I will come to the room after my shift and discuss the plans. Rose, is there anyone you know who lives in this area who can be trusted and could pose as a nurse?"

"Yes, I have my younger daughter with me. She can do whatever is needed."

"That's great; I will fill you in on the details after my shift."

Rose and David, filled with anticipation, quickly got dressed, both wearing baseball caps for extra coverage. Kimberley had declined her father's invitation to join them as she was more focused on mending fences with Stevin. Stephanie had advised that they all avoid visiting simultaneously.

Stephanie did as promised. Rose and David, their hearts filled with joy, got to hold the baby and take photos. David even Facetimed Stevin and Kimberley so they could share the moment. However, the time felt short-lived as Stephanie could only give them ten minutes with the baby.

When Stephanie and the ICU nurse pushed Summer by on the stretcher, Rose's knees buckled. The sight of her in that condition was too much to bear. Summer was fragile and thin and looked very unkempt. David clinched onto Rose's arm tightly as he felt her pulling away and walking towards Summer.

David knew it was time to remove Rose from the hospital, recognizing that seeing Summer was too overwhelming for her, encouraging her to return to the room with him and wait on Stephanie to advise them on their next move.

***

Stevin ignored the light tap on the door, his eyes rolling in the back of his head, feeling a surge of irritation that Kimberley would even attempt to speak to him.

"Stevin, please, I beg of you," Kimberley pleaded, her voice cracked with desperation. But Stevin, unmoved, remained resolute in his silence.

"Just give me five minutes, and you never have to speak to me again," she said, her forehead resting on the bedroom door.

Kimberley was startled as the door swung open, and Stevin stood in front of her in a scary demeanor. She quickly backtracked.

"Never mind," she said, feeling frightened by his presence.

For a brief second, it was like looking into Summer's eyes as he felt horrible for frightening her. He wasn't that monster.

"Wait, Kimberley," he said. "What do you need?"

"I understand if you never speak to me again, but I needed you to know I will never forgive myself for what I have put my parents and Summer through. So, you can hate me or never speak to me, but it will never equal my hate for myself and my actions."

Stevin let his guard down and looked at her with a soft expression. "Why, Kimberley, why would you not help her."

Kimberley burst into tears. "I don't know, Stevin, I don't know. I was so blinded by love that I honestly didn't know. Summer eyes haunt my every thought. I knew something wasn't right, but I wanted to believe him. I wanted to believe in us so badly that I was willing to walk away from everything. But I honestly believed him, Stevin, I truly did."

Stevin walked over and enveloped Kimberley in a hug. She then told him everything she had been doing to assist with Summer's search on her own.

***

The return to the hotel room was bittersweet, a whirlwind of emotions. Rose's body trembled with anxiety.

"David, I think we should just take our chance with the authorities."

David looked over at Stevin, surprised as he noted him sitting with Kimberley, having a civil conversation.

"Stevin, what do you think?"

Stevin hesitated for a brief moment, uncertainty flickering in his eyes. "Let's wait and see what Stephanie and Dr. Brown have planned. Summer once confided in me that Christopher attacked her while visiting his father here in California, and when she notified the police for help, Christopher made one call, and suddenly the officer removed her from the safety of his car and waled her over, handing her to Christopher like a prisoner."

Rose dropped her head, feeling defeated. "I will not leave California without my child and grandson!"

They all sat deep in thought when suddenly, there was a tap on the door, and it was Stephanie. She informed them she only had fifteen minutes on her break and didn't have much time. Stephanie told them Summer was awake and doing well and knew they were nearby. She instructed them that Summer had to be rescued first thing the following morning.

Kimberley was advised of her role as an unlicensed nursing student who would be completing her internship at the hospital. She would help them to assist with Summer's escape. Stephanie stood and took photos of Kimberley for her fake badge and instructed her to report to the 4th floor for her first day at 6:45 pm.

David and Rose were asked to rent a van, something large enough that Summer could recline and be comfortable traveling, as she wouldn't be able to fly. They would need to park on the hospital's south side behind the water tanks, out of sight of the cameras. Stephanie stressed the importance of them staying on course.

Stevin walked Stephanie out, his voice filled with longing as he asked if there was any way he could see Summer. Stephanie regretfully informed him that the bodyguards were back at Summer's door.

"We didn't think any of this out. Where would Summer and the baby go to ensure their safety? Rose asked. "We can't risk taking them back to Atlanta."

"Rose, get online and search for an RV dealership nearby?" David requested.

"David, we can't afford to purchase an RV," Rose said sadly.

"Mom, just search for it and provide me with the information related to cost and dealership. Summer and I have enough savings to purchase what we need. I will get my close buddy, Orlando, to buy it online, do a wire transfer, and put David as the pickup person.

"Money talks. With the right price, we can have it by the end of the day; just waive the walk-through. We just need to make sure the weight is under 26,000 pounds and no longer than 40 feet in length. We should be able to pull off the lot today. I took plenty of RV trips during my childhood, so I'm very experienced in the operations of RV's. But on that note, I need to run off; I need to take care of something, and I will be back," Stevin said.

"Where are you going, Stevin? We have a strict timeframe, and we need you to stay focused," David asked concernedly.

"I promise to return on time," Stevin said. "This is a matter that must be addressed," he said as he left the hotel room.

"Damn it, Rose. I knew bringing Stevin along could be a risk," David said, his face riddled with concern.

"Dad, I don't think Stevin would risk Summer's safety. Let's just focus on getting the RV," Kimberley suggested.

"Mom, I need to tell you something. I know where Summer could go and be safe," Kimberley said with concern. Kimberley stood in fear, knowing what she was about to reveal could very well backfire on her.

"Mom, I have been in contact with your father," she said in a low tone.

Rose's eyes widened as she stood, throwing her hands in the air, and charged towards Kimberley. David snatched her by the arm, pulling her back. Kimberley instantly closed her eyes, dug her toes into the carpet, and braced herself for another infamous slap.

Rose turned to David, her eyes blazing with fire. "Ask her why she hates me so much; what the hell have I done to that ungrateful brat to deserve this?" Rose said, staring at Kimberley with a dismissive flick of her eyes.

"Mom, I'm not trying to hurt you," Kimberley said as she dropped to her knees, crying, feeling defeated. She had lost everything, feeling there was nothing she could do to regain good grace with her mom.

David released Rose and hurried to Kimberley's side. Rose stood and watched Kimberley sob remorsefully for her actions. No matter how hurt and disappointed she was in her, this was still her baby girl panting on her knees, begging for her forgiveness.

"Kimberley, why would you contact your mom's father after she asked you not to?"

"Dad... I had nowhere to go—no one to turn to. When everyone found out what I did to Mom, no one would speak to me. I arrived in Minnesota with $100 in my bank account and my car on two spare tires. Papa Joe opened his doors to me. I told him how hurt and disappointed I was with him, and I was only there because I had nowhere to go."

"Kimberley, you know neither I nor your mother would allow you to be out on the streets. No matter how mad I was and still am, you are our child," David said, looking up at Rose as he cradled Kimberley in his arms.

"Kimberley's eyes shot up towards Rose. I didn't want you guys to help out of pity. I deserved everything I was going through. Mom and Summer didn't deserve what I did to them."

Rose backed away, taking a seat on the couch. "Mom, I didn't go to mend anything on your behalf. What your parents did to you is unthinkable, and I turned around and reopened your wounds, betraying you in the very same way. Your dad cries himself to sleep nightly with regrets of what he did to you. He has stacks of return letters he has been sending you for years. You have rejected all his mail."

David's eyes widened with surprise, looking up at Rose; he had no idea Rose's father knew her whereabouts. Rose's eyes darted towards Kimberley.

"Because he doesn't deserve my forgiveness, and I don't deserve having him pushed down my throat."

"No, Mom. It's the opposite. He has accepted that you will never talk to him, and he deserves that. He only encouraged me to fix what I had broken. He first paid for my trip to Illinois. I did what the detective told me; I learned who Summer was through the people she was close to. I even visited Summer's childhood home. I was given a large bag of cash to give to her. I don't think Mr. Jeffery's son knew what was in the oversized tote. I took a peek for myself.

"But Mom. Papa Joe knows everything he set in motion and what you and Summer has gone through. He has property and a business that's in the Richmond's name. You're the heir; you can pass it down to your kids if you don't want it. Your father stays twenty minutes from the property but continues running the small town store. He stepped away from the ministry after what he and your mom did to you. Papa Joe said he couldn't continue to preach the word when he had betrayed everything he stood for.

"Mom, you don't have to have contact with him; he just wants to mend what he broke. I have actually been staying on the property, traveling back and forth. Papa Joe has hired contractors to fix the house up located on the property. It's a large four-bedroom home. It only has minor issues, but we can drive from here. It will only take a day," she said, her voice filled with hope and desperation.

The room was silent as everyone sat deep in thought. Kimberley just wanted her overbearing, loving mother back, a mother who had been deeply hurt by her actions and had every right to be angry and disappointed with her.

Chapter: 5
The Ultimate Showdown

Stevin locked eyes with Stephanie as she walked past the nursery window. It was a different shift, so neither nurse would recognize him. He couldn't spot his little guy. He noticed Stephanie entering the stairwell when he followed.

"The baby is with Summer, Stevin. He is glued to her chest. She finally opened up; she is ready to fight. If our plan fails and we cannot rescue her using our current approach. In that case, we will involve the authorities and create enough attention that whoever's in his pocket will think twice before continuing to assist with Summer being held against her will."

"That's fine, Stephanie. As long as the baby is with her, I know his presence comforts her."

"She is eating him up, Stevin, he stares at her like he knows he is so loved."

"Stephanie, I need to check my email. Is there anywhere I can print some documents?"

"Yes, there is a public library next to the university a couple of blocks from here," Stephanie replied, gesturing toward the direction of the university.

Stevin exited the hospital as he used his phone and searched for a Medical Art Prosthetics store. He made several stops and collected a prosthetic nose and make-up to blend the silicone with his skin: a short grey wig and a pair of glasses.

He snapped a photo of himself using his cell phone after applying his disguise. He printed out the image and documentation his father's connections were able to provide. Making himself a fake ID, he leans back in the computer chair admiring his fake credentials, Dr. Harleen Quinzel, staff Psychiatrist.

Stevin arrived at the UCLA Mental Health Center parking lot, waiting for his contact to text with instructions. Mr. Bash had put

Stevin in touch with a staff member who worked in the psychiatric unit where Christopher was being treated.

His phone buzzed, snapping him out of deep thoughts. The message instructed Stevin to meet the contact at a side entrance on the west wing of the hospital's first floor. Christopher was located in a high-security unit. Mr. Diamond was afraid he would find a way to manipulate his way out of the hospital before he had proper treatment.

Stevin was instructed to follow his contact up the stairwell to the 9th floor. The contact expressed concern that Stevin might be stopped at the main entrance due to his unfamiliarity with the front desk security, as he would be perceived as a new staff member. It was emphasized that he would be required to sign in and present his credentials.

To avoid being noticed, they used the staff-only stairwell. Upon reaching the ninth floor, Stevin was directed to Christopher's room, which was the second on the right after the stairwell. He was advised to be aware of the camera, which only monitored the entrance of the doorway. He was also given a swipe card to exit the building after his visit.

Stevin was taken aback when he reached Christopher's room, which was very spacious and decorated like a hotel suite. Pausing, he leaned against the wall with his heart racing. The potential consequences of his actions weighed heavily on his mind, only heightening the suspense. If this visit went left, he could very well jeopardize Summer's escape. Fueled with anger, there was no way he wouldn't confront this psycho.

Knowing that Christopher wouldn't recognize him at first glance, he walked in, introduced himself as Dr. Quinzel, and asked Christopher to take a seat at the rectangular table in the room.

"What the fuck is this, another one of my father's flunkies," Christopher sneered, his tone oozing with superiority and arrogance.

"So, Mr. Diamond," he began. I'd like to ask about your childhood. "Did you have a troubled childhood? Did you have an abusive father?"

Christopher again scoffed, this time with an irritated laugh that betrayed his discomfort.

Stevin continued, "Was your father emotionally distant or mentally unstable?"

"You have about another minute before I throw you out of my room," Christopher threatened, but Stevin remained undeterred, his commitment to his mission unshaken.

"Do you like taking advantage of the weak?"

"What type of fucken question is that," Christopher spat in an angry tone.

"Hmm, from reading your file, I see Christopher Diamond, a 38-year-old male with a troubled past, is known for his abusive behavior and manipulative nature. So again, do you like to take advantage of women and force them into relationships with abuse and manipulation? My medical diagnosis would be an abusive narcissistic womanizer."

Feeling uneasy, Christopher sat up in his chair, his gaze locked with Stevin's as he studied his features. He couldn't shake the feeling that something was amiss about this visit.

Noticing Christopher's intense gaze, Stevin smiled and leaned back in his seat. But his smile faded, replaced by an angry expression as he realized Christopher was beginning to see through his facade.

"Good boy," he said, his voice tinged with disdain for Christopher.

Christopher chuckled, "A little weak man. You flew to California and even came in disguise to cry behind, what, my pussy!"

Christopher's arrogant laughter filled the room. "Man, move the hell on; my wife and my unborn child are at my family home waiting for Daddy to come home. And here you are whining over spilled milk that was never yours.

"How about this, let me call home and let you speak to Summer, oh, I mean my pregnant wife, so she can inform you how a real man gave it to her every night."

Christopher clearly hadn't been updated on Summer's condition or informed that the baby had been born, and Stevin's anger, seething revenge, was about to risk Summer's freedom and his newborn son.

Stevin, his eyes blazing with fury, stood and slowly backed away from the table, taking a few steps back towards the doorway to get in eye view of the camera. He eyed Christopher with a devilish smirk that twisted his features into a grotesque mask of malice.

"Oh, poor little Daddy's boy, really isn't Daddy's boy; he doesn't care about you either. If so, someone would have informed your delusional ass, you sad sack of shit, that my son was born two days ago.

"So, while you are here in the nut house, 'Little Crazy Man,' I'm on my way to pick up Summer and my son so we can carry on with our lives and treat you like the nonfactor you are."

Stevin's words had the desired effect, setting Christopher off. He launched himself from the table, charging towards Stevin with such force that their bodies slammed into the wall, with Christopher's arms bear-hugging Stevin around the waist. With both hands free, Stevin locked Christopher in a headlock while using his free arm diving his elbow into his side and back.

Christopher bit Stevin's side, causing him to scream out and release his neck. The two men threw blow after blow, as Stevin saw red with flashes of Summer's face going through his mind. With one solid right hook, Christopher dropped to his knees.

A nurse entered the room after hearing the commotion. Stevin yelled, "He attacked me with a pen!" The nurse quickly ran to the nurse's station and swiftly issued a Code Gray to room 902 via the overhead paging system. When she returned, Stevin had Christopher around the neck as Christopher struggled, screaming. "I'm going to kill this Son of a Bitch."

Stevin, posing as Dr. Quinzel, ordered stat Haldol 2mg and 1mg of Ativan. The nurse ran out of the room as the orderlies and medical staff entered, returning minutes later, injecting Christopher in his left deltoid. Christopher's attending doctor demanded answers as she pried Stevin's arm from around Christopher's neck.

Christopher was irate and continued charging at Stevin using threatening and vulgar language. He kept the staff busy as they wrestled to control him, giving Stevin an escape route. He ran down the stairwell and dashed out of the exit, leaving skid marks in the parking lot. With a sense of urgency, he pulled behind an abandoned building and swiftly changed the car's license plate back to its original one, then discarded the stolen tag and his disguise into a dumpster. Stevin, his heart pounding in his chest, called his dad, informing him of what he had done, and they made other plans to help Summer escape. If Christopher didn't remain sedated throughout the night and regain consciousness to inform his father of the circumstances, Stevin was prepared to go to war.

Meanwhile, Christopher's attending physician, Dr. Maria, demanded answers from the staff, as she demanded to know what happened, what medication the nurse had administered, and who gave the order. The hospital staff was clueless, and Christopher's nurse was visibly distraught as the identity of the unknown doctor remained a mystery.

Dr. Maria ordered a repeated low dose of Haldol every four hours to keep Christopher calm until she could investigate what had happened. She addressed the staff, emphasizing the potential consequences.

"Our professional positions are at risk, all of our jobs are in danger, that's if his father doesn't have us locked up and thrown under the jailhouse. Find out who that individual was and how he gained access into the facility, let alone my patient room," she demanded, knocking over items in the nurse's station, as she yelled, "Fuck Me!"

Tension mounted as David and Rose paced the room. Stevin had delivered as promised, and Orlando did, too. Thanks to his negotiating skills, David was able to drive off the RV lot 10 minutes before closing, despite the triple fee that was tacked on. They tackled one hurdle but now face another one, as Stevin's absence was a grave concern for them.

"Rose, call him again; he can't be this reckless. It's enough to stress placing Kimberley directly in harm's way; now we have to be concerned about Stevin's recklessness."

I have called David, but he's not picking up. Stephanie nor Kimberley has seen him around the hospital since earlier. Kimberley has texted every 30 minutes as promised. She even got to see Summer. She texted that Summer looked frightened when she walked in and clearly didn't trust her, but she didn't scream for help. She will return to her room and try to explain the situation when it's safe."

"Rose, try Stevin again, David demanded.

Stevin's cell phone could be heard ringing outside the hotel door. David snatches the door open. Stevin entered, face bruised, and shirt torn.

"What did you do, son? What did you do," David's voice rose, his frustration palpable as he threw his arms in the air, as if to say all their hard work had been compromised.

David couldn't bear to look at Stevin; he sat on the sofa, holding his head in his hands, attempting to calm down. Knowing blowing up on Stevin wouldn't help at that moment.

"Son," Rose said in a soft tone. Have you compromised Summer and your son's freedom?

"No, Mom, not at this precise moment," Stevin's response hung in the air, thick with uncertainty.

"What the hell does that mean, Stevin? I have both of my daughters across the street; both of their lives and freedom are in jeopardy. So, we need to know what you have done."

"Christopher will be..." Before Stevin could complete his sentence, David's disbelief turned into a furious outburst.

"Christopher, what do you mean, Christopher? You must be joking. You couldn't even control your emotions long enough to ensure the safety of your newborn son, and the woman you claim to love more than anything was safe out of harm's way. I just can't, I can't," David said as he stormed off to the bedroom.

"Stevin, do we need to inform Stephanie and Dr. Brown of the changes, that Christopher and his father are aware that you or Summer's family might be in town," Rose asked, her frustration evident as she attempted to keep her temper in check.

"No, Mom. I beat the shit out of him and made sure he was medically sedated and will remain medically sedated throughout the night. So, yes, we don't have any flexibility tomorrow. We must move out first thing in the morning as planned."

"Was it worth it, Stevin? Was it worth jeopardizing her safety?" Rose asked, standing and walking away disappointedly, leaving Stevin alone to sulk in his self-pity.

Breaking Free

Rose nervously stared at her watch, each second dragging by. The last communication she received from Kimberley was at 5 a.m., informing her that Summer was aware of the plan and that their only chance to escape was to exit the basement doors around 6:30 a.m. They were instructed to get to the RV and be ready to pull away as soon as she and Summer were spotted.

Stevin shouted, "I see them," jolting Rose out of deep thought. She was too afraid to look; she couldn't bring herself to look until both of her girls and grandson were safe and at the RV. She remained seated, praying until Kimberley could be heard screaming, "I got her mom. I got them."

Rose exploded through the RV door and was met by Kimberley, who handed her the oversized bag to remove baby Asher. It was as if time stood still for Rose as everything began to move in slow motion. Despite the urgency of the situation, she couldn't help but feel moved as she observed Stevin tenderly caressing Summer and expressing his love for her. David's urgent warning to Stevin snapped Rose out of her trance. "Son, we have to move," David said, his voice filled with concern and urgency.

Her New Home

After a grueling day and a half on the road, David and Stevin didn't get much sleep. Stevin struggled with being torn away from Summer, but he knew it was crucial that they drove without stopping. Besides, David couldn't shoulder the entire 29-hour trip alone.

Summer's eyes opened as she felt the change in the drive. The smooth interstate pavement became a rough, rocky movement as the RV shook with force. She glanced over Rose's shoulder as Rose stared out of the small RV window in curiosity as they reached their destination.

The rustic mountain house, which had a modern twist and appeared newly renovated, stood as a symbol of uncertainty. As Rose feared an unwelcome visit from her father, Summer's world teetered on the brink of collapse. She was haunted by the unknown, her fear of the Diamonds' sudden appearance and the potential loss of her son.

Everyone clung to Summer as they assisted her and the baby off the RV. Rose, her voice filled with concern, asked Stevin to carry Summer into the house. Summer couldn't help but harbor an extreme amount of guilt, knowing that it was because of her that everyone's life was turned upside down.

"No, Please don't! I don't want you all fussing over me. I can't even begin to fathom what this year has been like for either of you. I should have never involved you guys in this madness with Christopher. I'd rather walk; Stevin, just hold my hand, please."

"Nonsense! Listen, little missy, you're not going to tell me how to be a mother. You just went through one of the worst ordeals of your life, and let's not forget a traumatic birth that left you in a coma for a day. You don't get to tell us not to make a big fuss over you. Now, Stevin, pick her up and carry her onto the porch, onto even pavement, " Rose demanded.

"Sissy, get used to it; she's a smother bear," Kimberley said, bursting into laughter at her own corny joke, as no one else laughed. "You all get it, right, mommy bear, smother bear," she said as her laughter quickly faded.

Summer just smiled, feeling a warm wave of gratitude; it honestly felt nice to get fussed over by her mom, something she didn't get to experience as a child.

Kimberley showed everyone around the home. Stevin and Summer selected the primary bedroom located on the main floor to accommodate Summer's avoidance of stair climbing. Meanwhile, Rose, David, and Kimberley elected to occupy the second-floor bedrooms, aiming to offer Stevin and Summer their necessary privacy. The smaller first-floor bedroom was designated to serve as Asher's nursery.

Summer sat silently on the edge of the bed, her inner turmoil discernible. She should have been overjoyed and embracing Stevin, but instead, the weight of Christopher's actions made her feel unworthy of his love that she couldn't even look him in the eyes. How could she ever be worthy of his love after what Christopher did to her? He violated her in the worst way imaginable.

"Summer, are you ready for a shower, or do I have to sponge you off, being you have a surgical wound," Stevin asks.

"Uh...Uhhh," she stutters. "My mom can help me. Can you go get her for me?"

Stevin enters the family room, informing Rose that Summer is requesting her assistance with bathing. Rose then asks Kimberley to assist with the baby while she helps Summer. As the ladies left the room to assist Summer, David approaches Stevin, squeezing his shoulder.

He could see the disappointment and hurt all over Stevin's face. "Son, don't take it personally. Give her time. Summer has been through a lot, and we will never know what trauma she has endured. Her past PTSD has probably been magnified by a thousand. Just take it day by day, and please allow her to open up to you.

"Kimberley and I will be leaving tomorrow. Rose's dad has agreed to drive us to Iowa to catch a flight back home. I need to tie up some loose ends and take a leave from work. My and Sarah's home has sold, and I will be placing Rose's home on the market. Protecting my family will be much easier if I move them into my parents' home. I can't do this without getting my finances in order, so Rose will remain here, and Kimberley will assist me back home. I will counsel you and Summer when I return. Just be prepared; most of Summer's counseling will be solo, son, and this will be a battle for both of you. But Summer's healing can only happen when she allows it to."

"David, if it's money you and Mom need, Summer and I can assist. We have invested well."

"Thanks, son, but eventually, you and Summer will have your family to focus on, and I need to ensure Rose's, and my life doesn't crumble while helping you guys. The primary objective is to ensure that Christopher is brought to justice, allowing you and Summer to finally live free from his influence.

"Now, come on, son, let me take you on your first Daddy Day shopping trip. The baby will need some items to get you guys through."

"David, are you certain that we should proceed without the ladies? My knowledge of infant care is limited. I don't know anything about shopping for a baby."

"Come along, son; this is not my first rodeo."

CHAPTER: 7
HIS NEW REALITY

Stevin awoke to an empty bed. He could hear his son stirring in the bassinet as he smacked his lips, alarming Summer that it was time for his feeding. Inching to the edge of the bed, he sat deep in thought; he couldn't help but notice that Summer would pull away whenever he tried to touch or embrace her, even in the slightest way.

He was startled out of his thoughts when Summer spoke, asking if he could bring baby Asher so she could change and feed him. Sometime throughout the night, she had managed to retreat to the recliner on the other side of the room.

Stevin stood tall, his heart swelling with love and admiration as he gazed down at Asher. He took in every detail of his son's beautiful round face and tiny features, including his tiny, perfect lips as they stretched to yawn. For the first time in almost a year, he had a reason to smile, a reason to wake up every morning and start enjoying life. His family was finally together and complete.

After helping with a diaper change, he carefully handed Asher to Summer. Returning to the bed, Stevin sank into the mattress, his head swirling with emotion. "Summer, please don't shut me out," he pleaded.

"It's not intentional, Stevin. I can't express emotions that I don't fully comprehend and having a hard time processing myself."

"Summer, it's been damn near a year since you were last in my presence, and you left me alone in the bed and retreated to the chair."

Summer paused, her face a canvas of conflicting emotions. She sat up and carefully removed the baby from her breast as if she couldn't correctly nourish him while talking about Christopher. Gesturing for Stevin to take the baby, he gently placed him on his shoulder and slightly patted his small back to burp him.

Summer's every movement was a struggle as she eased herself to the edge of the cushion while using all her strength to push up.

Feeling the strain of her stitches, her lower abdomen tugged when she stood. Stevin offered to help and urged her to wait so he could assist her. She waved him off when he attempted to place the baby in his bassinet.

"No, Stevin, I'm okay. He needs to be burped before lying him down."

Summer wobbled over to the large bay window that offered a view of the neglected, overgrown garden. The early morning sunlight casting long, dappled shadows across the room. With a slight chuckle, she exhaled a deep breath—a breath filled with relief and gratitude for Stevin and her family, even Kimberley.

"I remember standing at the large window of the Diamond's estate, gazing at the impressive grounds. There was so much beauty in such a dark place. But to me, it was a prison; I thought my life was over. They threatened to take him and send me to jail for attempted murder if I didn't just walk away from him. That threat hung over me like a dark storm cloud daily, ready to break at any moment.

"Stevin, me leaving the bed last night had nothing to do with you. Christopher made me sleep in a spooning position every night, and some nights, with his hand positioned around my throat. So, forgive me, but some nights, I wake up, and it's hard to distinguish reality from my nightmares. I feel as if I'm suffocating."

"Are you saying you can't distinguish me from Christopher?" Stevin asked in a concerned voice.

"No, Stevin, that's not at all what I'm saying. I'm speaking about my reality and what I'm struggling through. Sweetheart, please don't make this personal. I can't pour into you if my cup is empty. I know my situation is asking a lot, and I also know you fulfill me in every way possible. All I asked is that you don't break while I'm going through this dark time."

"Never!" Stevin declared as he walked over to her, caressing her cheek.

Summer, unable to resist the pull at her heart, allowed his embrace. She turned her head slightly, resting it on his shoulder, a silent plea to Stevin not to cross her much-needed boundary. A boundary that was the only thing keeping her from falling into the dark abyss of her feelings. Although her heart ached with an intense longing for his touch, her mind held back, reminding her of her perceived unworthiness.

"Summer, Summer," Stevin called out, his voice filled with concern. He was standing, holding Summer in his arms, and she had utterly spaced out. His voice was only a distant murmur. He slightly shook her shoulders to snap her out of her daze. "Are you okay, Summer?"

"Yes, sweetie," she said in a low unconvincing tone.

"So, it's your time to be truthful. Are we going to keep skating around these bruises on your face and bite marks on your side?"

Stevin walked away with a wry smile and positioned himself near Asher, gently rubbing his jet-black curly hair. He then directed a cold gaze towards Summer and remarked, "Don't worry, he's in worse shape than I am."

Summer's eyes widened in surprise as she asked, "Who are you referring to, Christopher?"

"He's a psychotic pussy, Summer; I enjoyed beating the shit out of him. If it weren't for you and Asher, I would have broken his fucken neck."

"Christopher is in the hospital in a psychiatric unit. Please tell me you didn't do anything to jeopardize yourself, baby, or your freedom. I can't lose you."

"Don't you worry, your little pretty head, Miss Missy. Dr. Harleen Quinzel would never!" Stevin said, showing the photo he snapped of himself to make his fake badge.

Summer burst into laughter, "Well, Dr. Harleen Quinzel, let's just delete any evidence that connects you to an assault and battery."

Their much-needed laughter was interrupted by a video call from Stevin's parents. Stevin stiffened as he saw his mom's face planted directly on the phone. Knowing his Mother had no filter, he hesitated to answer.

"Hello, Mom. Dad, I can hardly see you. Mom, you have to back away from the phone," Stevin said, as she placed her entire face into the phone's camera, leaving only room for Mr. Bash's shoulder.

"Yeah...yeah...yeah," Mrs. Irene said, her voice carrying a hint of sarcasm as she demanded to see her grandchild. Stevin walked over to Asher's bassinet, allowing his parents to finally lay eyes on their grandson since leaving the hospital.

Mrs. Irene belted out a nursery rhyme in Italian, causing Asher to thrash and smack for his next meal.

"Hold on, Mom. Let me hand him to Summer. He's in search of his next meal." Summer held the baby up, allowing a good view with his eyes open. His senses heightened as he became more alert when he smelled her breast milk.

"Hello, Mrs. Irene," Summer said, but she received no response. Mr. Bash, Sr. quickly spoke, asking Summer how she was doing. The conversation ended swiftly as baby Asher showed his parents and grandparents how well his lungs actually worked, demanding to be fed.

Stevin could see the doubtful look on Summer's face when he kissed her forehead. "I'm assuming she knows everything, huh," Summer asked. As it was evident, Mrs. Irene purposely avoided talking to Summer, adding another layer of tension to the already strained family dynamics.

Feeling the weight of the situation wearing on him, Stevin abruptly halted the conversation. "Summer, I'm exhausted dealing with the situation at hand. My mother will adjust," he stated wearily.

His exhaustion was palpable, and Summer could sense the strain he was under. Despite her own feelings of unworthiness due to Christopher's actions and her belief that Stevin should share those sentiments towards her, she realized that she needed to accept that Stevin's feelings were not hers to dictate. She couldn't bear to lose him again and was determined to mend the rifts caused by her past in every relationship.

Summer was painfully aware that Mrs. Irene harbored a deep dislike for her. Not only was she aware of it, but Mrs. Irene also shared Summer's situation, often exaggerating or misrepresenting it, with every family member who would lend an ear.

CHAPTER: 8
THE DIAMOND'S WRATH

Los Angeles Health Medical Center

The Day of the Escape: Stephanie pushed baby Asher's bassinet to the far back of the nursery, hoping the nursery nurse would complete his assessment last. To ensure this, she distracted the nursery nurses by bragging about her home basketball team winning the game over the Lakers later that evening. Hearing a loud knock on the nursery window, she looked up and caught a glance at Mr. and Mrs. Diamond. Her breath caught in her throat. She hurriedly exited the nursery, but Mr. Diamond stopped her.

Before Stephanie could fully process the situation, Mr. Diamond's abrupt and accusatory voice cut through the air. "Young lady, is it customary for the medical staff to ignore family members?" he asked, his tone laced with rudeness.

Stephanie's mind raced with fear and anxiety, but she forced herself to maintain a calm exterior. "I'm sorry for the wait, but we are currently in the middle of a shift change. I'm sure they are not ignoring you. The showcase window will reopen once the babies' assessments are complete. You are more than welcome to return to the patient room, as the babies will immediately be returned to the mother's bedside. You will not only get a chance to see the baby but also to hold your new little family member," Stephanie said, holding her breath as she walked off.

Struggling to keep her fear in check, Stephanie dashed down the stairwell. She threw herself against the door, her heart racing with terror. Her only thought was to reach the hospital's south side and ensure Summer's safety. Before she could steady herself and climb the stairs to the 8th floor, which had a large showcase window that overlooked the back of the hospital parking lot, her phone dinged.

She received a text from Rose: "*Stephanie, we got her. Thank you and Dr. Brown for everything you have done. I know you guys risked a lot. I will reach back out when it's safe.*"

Stephanie sighs in relief. Now, she must gather herself and return to the unit. She knew that the discovery of the doll in the bassinet and Summer's and the baby's absence would set off a series of events.

***

Brody sat up so abruptly in his chair that it seemed as if he had been jolted awake, hesitating for a moment before finally rising to greet Mr. and Mrs. Diamond.

"Hello, Brody; any news to report?" Mr. Diamond's imposing figure loomed over Brody, his voice sending shivers down Brody's spine. Brody was acutely aware that Mr. Diamond was not pleased with him. Just a few days earlier, he had defied a direct order from him by refusing to enforce a directive to make Summer go visit Christopher, resulting in his temporary removal from duty.

"No, sir. I am just waiting for Summer to return from some tests."

"What the hell do you mean waiting on her? Your orders were to remain with her at all times," Mr. Diamond's stern tone was like a whip, causing Brody to instinctively shrink back into his seat.

"Sir, when I came on duty, I was informed that Dr. Santos had ordered some tests, and only staff were allowed to enter the restricted area."

"So, it never occurred to you to wait outside the doors on the floor where she was being transferred?"

Mr. Diamond's temporal throbbing intensified as he pushed past Brody and entered Summer's hospital room. Anxious and unsettled, he paced around, sensing that something was amiss, his every step echoing a feeling of dread settling in. Frantically, he dialed Dr. Santos on his cell phone, demanding to know about the test ordered for Summer.

Dr. Santos, his confusion evident in his voice, seemed unaware of any test being ordered. He stated that he was walking into the hospital, headed to the unit, and would follow up with Dr. Brown. Mr. Diamond requested Dr. Santos to call the nursery and have the nurse bring the baby to Summer's hospital room immediately.

Mrs. Diamond, oblivious to what might be happening, remained outside the door, chatting with Brody as he boasted about how adorable her brand-new grandson was.

After what felt like an eternity of nervous anticipation, Mr. Diamond burst through the door, startling his wife.

"Honey, what's the matter? You need to be patient. I know you're eager; we both are," she reassured him.

"No, darling, something isn't right," Mr. Diamond declared as he strode purposefully toward the nursing station. Mrs. Diamond and Brody quickly followed suit, their hearts pounding with concern.

"Brody, which one of these nurses escorted Summer off the unit?"

Brody's eyes darted around the nurse's station; his brow furrowed in concentration. "The nurse isn't present," he said, his voice tinged with worry.

Mr. Diamond scuffed in anger, his frustration boiling over. Brody's shout pierced the air, and he pointed, "That's one of the nurses," as Stephanie emerged from the stairwell.

"Oh, Shit! Take a deep breath and stay calm; you got this, she kept repeating to herself. How can I assist you?" Stephanie asked.

Mr. Diamond walked off quickly, his footsteps echoing with each rushed step. He noticed that every time something went wrong with the orders he or Dr. Santos gave, that particular nurse was always present. He reached the nursery window and noticed the confused look on the nurses' and Dr. Santos' faces. Dr. Santos could be seen speaking with the nurse when they both looked up at the Diamonds simultaneously. The nurse immediately took the bassinet sheet and threw it over the bassinet, which was labeled Diamond.

Dr. Santos wheeled the bassinet out of sight from the nursery window. Mr. Diamond began banging on the nursery door. Dr.

Santos quickly opened the door and said, "Nate, please, I need you to calm down."

"What the hell is going on," Mr. Diamond shouted.

Ushering the Diamonds into the nursery, they were led to a private room. With each second, their anticipation grew, until they finally stood before the bassinet that cradled their heir.

Mr. Diamond slowly pulled the sheet from the baby bassinet that covered their grandson. A moment of stunned silence passed as Mrs. Diamond gasped and covered her mouth. "Is my grandson... dead?" she whispered, her voice trembling as she buried her face into her husband's chest.

Mr. Diamond struggled to comprehend what he was seeing. The figure in the bassinet resembled a baby and was dressed as one, but its stiffness was eerily reminiscent of a lifeless body.

With a mixture of confusion and disbelief, he lifted the motionless form with one hand before dropping it back into the bassinet. "What the hell is this?" He scuffed.

Mrs. Diamond, still reeling from shock, jolted her head up with a bewildered expression when Mr. Dimond dropped their grandson's limp body into the bassinet.

"It's a doll," Dr. Santos declared softly, lowering his head.

"A doll?" the Diamonds exclaimed in unison, their voices a blend of astonishment and disbelief.

"I want this hospital shut down immediately! Call the authorities and locate Summer now!" Mr. Diamond ordered.

"Nate, we can't do either," Dr. Santos informed him.

"What the hell do you mean? Have you lost your mind? I'll call them my damn self," Mr. Diamond declared, while Mrs. Diamond, her face a mask of disbelief, stood by.

Dr. Santos quickly snatched Mr. Diamond's phone from his ear, leaving him in disbelief.

"No, Nate, have you forgotten the circumstances? Do I need to remind you of how many laws we have broken?"

"Summer is the only one who needs to be worried about breaking the law, not us; she just kidnapped my grandson."

"Dammit, Nate, we held her hostage for months. Hell, you parked armed bodyguards at her door daily while she was an inpatient. Let alone when she was admitted, she had been beaten to near death. Do you know how many calls administration received from concerned nurses about Summer's condition? Anonymous complaints came up daily about a young pregnant woman being held against her will. We blocked and buried every complaint on your behalf. Besides, Summer hasn't broken any laws. The baby was clear for discharge, but Summer wasn't. It's not illegal for a mother to leave the hospital with her newborn before being discharged. If Summer decides to come after us, not only am I facing prison time, but she can sue this facility for false imprisonment. This hospital can be held liable for everything I have opened the doors to.

"I have alerted security, and they are currently searching the hospital grounds for Summer and the baby. Unfortunately, the cameras on this floor have been down for a week now. Depending on when Summer left the grounds, we might never know. Our IT department recently conducted a system upgrade, and for 30 minutes, the entire hospital security system was down for maintenance."

Mr. Diamond stood in disbelief, consumed by anger. Throughout his adult life, he had always maintained control. The thought that an orphan, who he perceived as lacking intelligence and blindly compliant- a simple yes woman- could manipulate him and his family, thus sullying the reputation of the Diamond family name, was inconceivable.

"Peter, it seems you have forgotten who I am. So, let me remind you. I will decide whether you continue to practice or if I want to wash my ass with your medical degree. What I do know is that Summer couldn't pull this off by herself, so that tells me that your staff is up to this in their eyeballs—summoned every nurse on this unit for an interview. Including that Doctor Brown." The tension in the room was so thick it could be cut with a knife.

"Nate, I can request that the nurses come in and answer some questions, but I cannot demand that Dr. Brown come in and be unofficially interrogated."

Dr. Santos dropped his head as Mr. Diamond stared at him with rage in his eyes, only snapping out of his cold stare when his phone rang. The sudden interruption of the phone call from Christopher's doctor at UCLA Mental Health Center broke the intense moment, as Dr. Santos feared for his career.

Dr. Santos felt relieved when Mr. Diamond answered his phone, a quick distraction from his rage, but his sense of relief quickly turned to concern as Mr. Diamond's voice erupted as he could be heard shouting," What the hell do you mean a staff member attacked my son?" After expressing his frustration towards the doctor on the call, Mr. Diamond demanded the immediate release of his son, Christopher.

Before turning his attention back to Dr. Santos, he made several calls, issued a flurry of orders, and mobilized his staff to the hospital to aid in the search for Summer and his grandson. In addition, he instructed his top private investigator to launch an extensive inquiry into Summer, her family, and any suspicious hospital staff, with specific attention directed toward Stephanie and Dr. Brown.

Mr. Diamond swiftly pivoted his focus back to Dr. Santos.

"When I return, I expect to interview every staff member who worked last night and the staff on duty now," he said as he swiftly left the nursery, guiding Mrs. Diamond out the door.

They passed by Brody, who was waiting for his next orders. Stopping abruptly, Mr. Diamond swiftly turned to Brody and said, "You are relieved of duty, indefinitely! As for your wife, inform her that her services are no longer needed either."

Brody's mouth flew open, and Mrs. Diamond stood in shock; she wanted to protest her husband's orders, but she remained silent and stared at Brody with teary eyes. The apple didn't fall too far from the tree. The difference between Pamala Diamond and Summer is that she knew her place and did not defy her husband's orders.

CHAPTER: 9
VENGEANCE IS MINE

Christoper Release

"Christopher, can you recall the events that occurred on yesterday?"

"I don't know how many times I have to tell you, nincompoops, I wasn't attacked, or no one attacked me."

"Christopher, I know that isn't true. I'm not sure why you are denying the incident, but it won't extend your stay if that's what you are worried about. Your father has already requested your immediate release. He is your medical proxy, so nothing you say changes my discharge orders," Dr. Maria stated with a calm yet assertive tone, her eyes fixed on Christopher.

"Well, I'm sorry, doc. The last thing I remember is losing my balance from these unnecessary sedative meds you guys keep pumping in me." Christopher replied, his frustration evident in his voice.

"So, Christopher, you're suggesting that these bruises on your face and body are the result of a simple fall?" Dr. Maria's tone was laced with skepticism, and her eyes were fixed on Christopher.

Christopher failed to respond, drooping his head and rubbing his bruised chin. Dr. Maria paused, slowly closing Christopher's chart. She knew he was full of shit. The question lingered in her mind: why? If his silence kept his father off her ass, she could care less about his mysterious amnesia.

Relieved when his interrogation was over, he seethed in anger. He indeed remembered every second of his encounter with Stevin, and vengeance was his. No doctor, the authorities, and especially his father would take that moment from him; Stevin belonged to him, and he would suffer the consequences. As far as Summer, he made her a promise: if she ever crossed him again, he would make her watch as he destroyed everything and everyone she thought she loved. Christopher was determined to keep that promise.

Mr. Diamond's eyes widened in disbelief as he stepped into Christopher's room. "You have got to be shitting me," he exclaimed. His mom's hands flew to her mouth as she took in the sight of her son's bruised face, and tears welled up in her eyes.

Mr. Diamond hurried to the nurse's station, desperate for answers. Tension filled the air as Dr. Maria was urgently paged to Christopher's room. She entered the room with purpose, carrying a laptop, and began to weave a tale about a first-year intern who had been mistakenly assigned to Christopher's room. She showed the security footage, which captured a brief moment of the incident when Stevin came into view of the camera. All that could be seen was Christopher charging at the medical staff.

"Dad, I can't stay here any longer. I don't know anything about that video. I keep telling you they keep giving me these unnecessary psychotic meds that make me trip and fall. I'm ready to go home, and I don't want anything she's prescribing; look at my face. You see what being in their care equals to. Just be grateful I'm still breathing."

The atmosphere crackled with unspoken questions and unease. Mr. Diamond felt overwhelmed by the sudden turn of events as he followed Dr. Maria back to the nursing station. Still processing the news of his grandson's birth and now his disappearance left him reeling. He wanted to avoid Christopher's disruptions, as he wanted nothing to do with Dr. Maria's discharge orders. He needed to keep him calm, knowing he had more disturbing news to deliver.

Mixed with a potent blend of anger and hurt, Christopher confronted his mother, "Mom, my son was born three days ago, and nobody thought to tell me."

"Son, your father and I were on vacation. We only arrived back in the states this morning. Summer was rushed to the hospital and had to have an emergency cesarean. It was enough worrying about the baby's safety; we didn't want to put you through the stress, knowing we couldn't get you released, until our return. Your father and I will discuss the matter once we arrive home."

The car ride back to his parents' home was dreary. He hated his childhood home just as much as his disdain for Stevin. The atmosphere became increasingly tense, as his parents made him wait until they arrived back at the family home before telling him the status of his son and Summer.

Although he knew there was a good chance Summer's child wasn't his, nothing gave him more pleasure than ripping Stevin's son out of his life.

As they gathered around the polished oak table, Christopher sensed the impending news wouldn't be in his favor. His father, a man of strict principles and a stickler for table manners, had broken his own number one rule by resting his elbows on the table while burying his face in his hands. The weight of guilt consumed him, and he seemed to be grappling with a profound sense of failure towards his son.

"Son, Summer disappeared from the hospital, taking your son." Mr. Diamond murmured, his head dropping, unable to meet Christopher's gaze.

Christopher's lips curled into a triumphant smirk as he gazed at his father. He felt a surge of satisfaction, relishing the rare moment of seeing his usually authoritative father humbled at his feet, a silent moment of victory. An urge to challenge his father's decisions bubbled up inside him, prompting the thought to shout, "Sit up, Father, and remove your elbows from the table. I see the mighty Nate Diamond has stumbled, and didn't know what was best for my life." As he rose from his seat and paced around his father, lost in his triumph. Christopher was suddenly snapped back to reality by his mother's gentle touch. "Darling, did you hear your father?"

Christopher eased back into his seat; his gaze turned blank as he looked at his father. "Summer and my son are my concerns. There's no need to involve yourselves any longer in this matter; I will handle Summer as I see fit."

"Like hell, you will," Mr. Diamond retorted with a derisive tone. I've had my fill of this mess you've caused over the past year. I'm up to my neck in the bullcrap you have created. You better pray like hell, Summer remains a mute mouse without a voice. I risked Peter and the entire Los Angeles Health Medical Board covering up your psychotic behavior. I imprisoned this young woman for you! What goes on through your head, son?" His voice thundered through the room as he called Christopher out on his behavior.

Christopher was seemingly unfazed, ignoring his father's demands as he stood up and excused himself from the table.

"Pam, that boy isn't well. I can't continue bailing him out. He's going to ruin the family name, if he doesn't destroy me first," Mr. Diamond said with a furrowed brow, deep in thought as he contemplated his next move. He knew he needed to find Summer before Christopher did, realizing the urgency of the situation.

CHAPTER: 10
THE INTERROGATION ROOM

Christopher looked out the window of his childhood bedroom, watching his mother say goodbye to his father as his private driver chauffeured him away.

The grand corridor of the mansion felt eerily quiet and lonely, stirring memories of his troubling childhood. His parents had no room to judge, both grappling with their own demons. His mother, a recovering alcoholic, drank herself into submission. Or perhaps it was the result of his father's oppressive hold over her, a desire to maintain the family's facade of normalcy, keeping her confined in a guest bedroom instead of seeking professional care in her worst state, which she desperately needed the most. There was no way his father would let the world know his mom was a drunk, shielding her struggles.

Instead, she was locked away at a time during Christopher's childhood when he needed her the most. The echoes of her sorrowful screams and desperate pleas to be set free haunted his thoughts. His brothers would be ordered by their father to drag him to his room and away from her bedroom door, where he would curl up next to it, weeping for her and enduring her pleas to be set free.

The situation was filled with bitter irony as he realized that his father had confined Summer to the same room. The door had remained shut ever since she was taken away. Throughout Summer's stay, the staff had been strictly prohibited from entering, causing the housekeeper to avoid the room unless given explicit orders from the Diamonds.

Lost in contemplation, he stood outside the closed bedroom door when the sound of his ringing phone shattered the silence.

"This is Jeff. I received your text, Christopher," he said, his voice filled with annoyance.

"Yes, Jeff, I need you to retrieve some information for me. I'm aware that, through my father's dealings, you have a contact who can access patients' medical records at L.A.H."

"No, Christopher, that's a no-go. I have direct orders from your father not to assist you with any investigation unless he approves it, and I haven't received any orders from him regarding you."

Christopher chuckled. "Hmm, I see. Jeff, I'm assuming you didn't think I was aware you ran back to my father and delivered him every file I requested of you. So, I also assume you thought you were safe because I haven't sold your conniving ass out to my father. But you see, from one wise man to another, I own you.

"Now, unless you want me to inform my father, your irresponsible and unreliable brother was the primary reason his company was audited by the IRS, costing him millions. It's vital for you and your family that you adjust your tone when speaking to me. So you see, I figured an eye for an eye. I just need to know how far along my wife was when she delivered my son; it is such a simple request. And by the way, Jeff, this conversation needs to be kept between us," Christopher said in a low tone, afraid of being heard.

"Christopher, I don't do well with threats. Make this your last time contacting me," Jeff said sharply, his voice laced with tension, before abruptly ending the call. The two men had a lengthy history of working together, but their relationship was far from amicable.

With a sly smile, he shook his head, realizing Jeff had hung up on him. It was no sweat off his back; he knew Jeff would deliver.

Christopher's brief conversation with Jeff had interrupted his need to see the room Summer had occupied while living with his parents. He entered the bedroom, his heart throbbing with sorrow. The bedroom still carried Summer's natural scent, and her last worn shirt laid across the bed. He picked it up, taking a big sniff as he lay across the bed with the shirt draped over his face. Memories of their intimate moments—the warmth of her body, the softness of her touch—flooded his mind with such vividness that it was almost as if she was there with him, making him ache for her presence.

As he moved, his head brushed against something solid under her pillow. Pulling out a book, he realized it was Summer's diary. When he opened the diary, a photo of Summer slipped from its pages and landed softly on the bedspread.

Brody's wife, Harmony, had persuaded Summer that she needed a picture to remind her of her pregnancy. Without the Diamond's knowledge, Harmony had secretly taken the photo and got it printed.

In the photograph, Summer stood on the lush, sprawling grounds of his parent's estate, her hands gently cradling her sizeable, round belly. The soft sunlight bathed the scene in a warm glow, yet her face appeared tense, reflecting a strain that hinted at her discomfort. It seemed as though she had been forced to pose for the moment, which robbed the photo of its authenticity. Nothing about the photo conveyed that she was a happy, expecting new mother.

He began reading Summer's diary. Each page spoke of her resilience, filled with lines that repeated, "I am a survivor. I am loved." Christopher felt a lump in his throat as overwhelming guilt washed over him; she was his delicate, innocent rose—his symbol of purity and grace. He had to accept that he was solely responsible for her resentment towards him. If only he had allowed her to keep their baby, they could have been married and living a happy life in Bora Bora. Instead, his anger had consumed him, leading to a moment of rage that cost him everything.

Christopher's phone dinged, alarming him to a new text. With a trembling hand, he wiped away his tears, which had blurred his vision. He blinked rapidly, trying to focus on the document he had just received from Jeff.

The words on the screen stood out starkly: 'Full-term delivery newborn was >=39 weeks of gestation at the time of birth.'

Christopher was well aware that if there were any chance of Summer's son being his, the baby would have likely been delivered preterm, around 34 to 36 weeks of gestation. In a surge of frustration and anger, he flung his phone onto the bed, snatched up the photo of

Summer, and tore it to shreds. Shifting his head in a grotesque intensity, he positioned his ear to hear the photo as it ripped apart, piece by piece. Each tear of the paper sounded like a small, mournful whisper as it met his ears, and he pressed his face closer, almost as if he were attempting to hear the fragments of their memories unraveling.

After a lingering moment, he closed his eyes slowly, allowing the weight of his emotions to wash over him like a heavy tide. His breaths became deliberate and deep, as if he needed to draw strength from the air itself, grounding himself amid the chaos of his thoughts. Suddenly, his eyes snapped open with an almost unnatural quickness as if he were possessed. Christopher surged to his feet as if driven by an unseen force. In his mind, Summer was weak; she had allowed the enemy to invade and permeate what was once pure. His love for her instantly turned into revenge, and he vowed vengeance would be his!

***

Mr. Diamond strode into the conference room with a visible disdain directed at Dr. Santos, who had informed him for the second time before returning to the hospital that he was not willing to summon any of the doctors into a meeting to be interrogated. The urgency of the situation was underscored by the visible tension between the two.

Amy, the nursery nurse, had allowed Stevin a private visit and permitted him to spend time with the infant in a secluded room within the nursery. Despite adamantly denying witnessing anything suspicious and claiming that no visitors were noted for baby Diamond, Amy's dishonesty would be difficult to prove. She was aware that the individual posing as the infant's father had not signed in, leaving no record of his presence. She also knew that the surveillance cameras were offline. Any attempt to prove her dishonesty would require substantial evidence and she was certainly not forthcoming with any additional information.

Rayla entered the conference room, exuding an unmistakable air of defiance, her attitude boldly expressed on her face. As an agency nurse working at multiple facilities, her lack of respect for upper management was evident. Her exhaustion was palpable; her eyes were heavy, as if burdened by sleepless hours, having just fallen asleep before being summon back to work. She plopped down in the chair and nonchalantly popped her gum with a casual disregard for the seriousness of the meeting.

Dr. Santos began by asking Rayla to state her name.

"Rayla Thomas," she replied, punctuating her name with a loud pop of her gum while rolling her eyes. "Excuse me, I don't mean to be rude, but can somebody please explain the purpose of this meeting and why I am being questioned?"

"Well, Ms. Thomas, one of your patients went AWOL sometime this morning while you were on duty, taking her baby with her and leaving a doll in the infant's place. I can see that you were the nurse responsible for caring for Mrs. Diamond," Dr. Santos explained, his tone serious.

"Yes, sir. Mrs. Diamond was one of my patients with whom I shared care with the trainee I was assigned," Rayla explained.

"May I have the name of your trainee," Dr. Santos inquired."

"Her name was Kimberley."

"What is her last name?" Mr. Diamond interjected abruptly; his sudden question prompted a stern look from Dr. Santos. "Peter, I don't see a Kimberley listed here before us."

"I don't know," Rayla said with a roll of her neck. "Knowing a coworker's middle or last name is not my job. Her name was assigned to me on the board. It was written as KIM-BER-LEY," she added, as the sight of Mr. Diamond started to make her stomach churn.

"That's okay, Rayla. We have several interns assigned to your unit. I will follow up with HR to obtain that information. I noticed that at 2:16 AM, you added a telephone order to the patient MAR, per my request?"

"Actually, Kimberley took the call while I was attending to another patient, receiving assistance from another nurse. I permitted her to log into the system using my badge—a standard practice we follow when a trainee is in the learning phase. I showed her how to place an order for a CT scan of the abdomen due to complications from surgical hemorrhaging," Rayla clarified.

"Peter, am I hearing this correctly? Earlier, you mentioned that you did not give any orders for Summer to leave this floor."

Dr. Santos leaned in, speaking in a low tone, "Nate, you have to control yourself." The looks he started to garnish from Rayla made Dr. Santos uncomfortable to carry on with questioning the staff. "No, I did not give this order, and neither did my PA."

Mr. Diamond's hand forcefully struck the table as he stood up from his seat. "Are you seriously telling me that your nurses are so incompetent that they would follow any random order from anyone who wants to call this hospital and pretend to be a doctor and give a fake order?"

Dr. Santos bowed his head, struggling to comprehend how his friend could place him in such a predicament.

"I'm sorry, Dr. Santos, but I cannot proceed with this meeting without a representative from my agency present. We have multiple doctors calling this unit throughout the night and issuing orders. It is not the responsibility of the nurses to authenticate the credentials of the doctor, especially when calling and using the staff name. If I were to decline to acknowledge a doctor's directive, demanding that they undergo an inquiry prior to receiving a verbal directive from my superior, I would undoubtedly jeopardize my employment. The last interaction I had with Mrs. Diamond was at approximately 0600. I conducted a bedside assessment and informed her that the baby would need to be returned to the nursery for shift change. She requested to breastfeed her infant first. Given Stephanie's familiarity with the patient and Kimberley's assistance with Mrs. Diamond's care, I allowed her to complete the bedside shift report with the returning nurse. Kimberley did not return to the nurse's station after giving Stephanie report," Rayla stated as she stood to leave.

Dr Santos leaned forward, his voice firm as he affirmed, "You are correct, Rayla. I am not requesting that you scrutinize the doctors."

"Like hell you shouldn't," Mr. Diamond's voice boomed, interrupting the conversation with a clear struggle for authority in his tone. "Young lady, this meeting isn't over."

"That's it, Nate! I couldn't walk into your office and speak to your staff in such a manner," Dr. Santos shouted, his frustration evident.

"You seem to be more worried about this gutter rat's feelings rather than locating my grandson."

Rayla's mouth flew open as she stormed out of the conference room, attempting to close the large conference door forcefully.

"That's it, Nate. You have tied my hands. The interviews are over."

"Oh, Peter, calm down. This is a delicate matter for me. My family is in disarray. Are we not friends?" Mr. Diamond inquired.

With a heavy sigh, Dr. Santos drops his head and begins to organize the papers on the table. "Nate, I'm not sure what the hell we are. I will allow Stephanie to be interviewed, but keep in mind that Stephanie is a veteran at this facility and speaking to her in that tone you just pulled with that young lady will not fly with me."

Mr. Diamond reclined in his chair, seemingly indifferent to the demands directed at him. Dr. Santos used the phone in the conference room, swiftly dialing the nurses' station and summoning Stephanie.

As Stephanie enters, she tries to maintain a facade of confidence. She walks over and extends her hand to Mr. Diamond, but he refuses. Dr. Santos quickly gets up from his seat, shakes her hand, and guides her to a chair.

Stephanie proceeded to recount the events, explaining that she had received a report from the intern, Kimberley, regarding Summer's scheduled CT scan at 0630. She described how she had assisted in obtaining a wheelchair for Summer and then waited outside the room, speaking with the security while Kimberley assisted Summer. Upon entering the room, she observed Kimberley placing the infant into the glass bassinet. She detailed how Kimberley verified the infant's ID bracelet on the ankle while she read out loud the ID number for Mrs. Diamond's wrist bracelet. The infant was smacking and making noises when Kimberley pushed the bassinet towards her, and they both left the room in opposite directions as she walked back to the nursery with Mrs. Diamond's security. She only realized something was wrong when Mr. Diamond stormed into the nurses' station.

In a fit of rage, not believing a word Stephanie said, Mr. Diamond lunged at her, demanding the truth. Dr. Santos quickly intervened, asking Stephanie to leave the conference room while he had to physically restrain Mr. Diamond. The tension escalated as they tugged at each other's shirts, with a sense of betrayal hanging in the air. Mr. Diamond threatened to end Dr. Santos's career before storming out of the room. Dr. Santos eased down in his chair, staring deep into the ceiling, coming to the realization that his career was in jeopardy and his freedom was at risk. The most frightening realization of them all was that he had crossed Mr. Nate Diamond!

CHAPTER: 11
STARTING OVER

Summer's eyes slowly fluttered open as the gentle warmth of the rising sun kissed her face. Blinking away the remnants of sleep, she sought reassurance in the golden light, yearning to believe that her freedom and the promise of happiness were not merely fragile illusions that would crumble into darkness. Her heart ached with the weight of her internal struggle, a battle she fought every morning.

She awoke daily to an intense sense of guilt. For the last two weeks, Stevin had retreated to the room designated for Asher's nursery. He couldn't mentally take Summer's rejection anymore, a routine that had become all too familiar.

Stevin and Asher seemed to wake up almost simultaneously every morning as if their internal alarm clocks were perfectly synchronized. Despite giving Summer her space, Stevin didn't miss a morning being the first face Asher saw, as his adorable little stretches were impossible to resist.

In her own way, Summer prioritized supporting Stevin's special bonding moments with Asher. Every morning, she would remain in bed, allowing Stevin the opportunity to be the first to embrace their son. As he changed Asher's diaper, his hands skillfully and confidently managed the task while cradling him in his arms, relishing those precious moments before handing Asher over for his morning feeding. Summer was fully aware that these moments together were strengthening their family bond. A connection she felt she lacked and was incapable of providing to Stevin but witnessing their moments helped ease the weight of her guilty conscience.

Stevin entered the bedroom and tiptoed to the bassinet, where Asher lay awake, with his eyes wide open, fixed on him as if he knew his dad would be there. Stevin was completely captivated by his son's enduring gaze and failed to notice that Summer was also awake. Sensing her gaze, he looked up to find Summer smiling and gushing over what she was seeing.

"Why are you smiling so big this morning? " Stevin inquired as he walked over to the bed to hand off Asher.

"My man, my man, my man," she said in a lighthearted manner. "Fatherhood looks so sexy on you," she remarked with a radiant smile.

Returning the smile, Stevin leaned in to kiss her forehead. While he appreciated her warm gesture, and it was nice that she could look at him and smile, his reality differed significantly from her sudden gesture at that moment.

"You know that I am meeting Pop today? Camille and her husband will follow him while he drives your car. I have to head out soon. Dad will assist me with connecting the tow bar so I can bring the car back here.

"Summer, it's a day trip. I thought it would be a great opportunity for you and the baby to accompany me. This way, my father and cousin can also meet him. It's a chance for us to spend some alone time together and for you to rebuild that bond with my family."

"Stevin, it's important that we don't forget. Moms, Dad, or whatever we're calling him, has assisted with setting up an appointment for the baby to receive his vaccinations first thing in the morning. We need to ensure we are there for this appointment. Apparently, this whole town is teeming with relatives from his side. The local pediatrician happens to be Mom's first cousin, with whom she grew up with. She will aid in obtaining Asher a birth certificate, as she will be registering his birth as a home birth in this county."

"Oh...I forgot," Stevin said with a long face and disappointing eyes. "Summer tread lightly when speaking about your grandfather. I'm not a fan of the guy myself, but we are currently living on his property."

"Yeah, about that. Listen, Stevin. I have no problem with you are mom having a relationship with him. But for me and my son, we will never, which brings me to my next point. I think we should do a paternity test for Asher."

"I don't need a damn blood test to tell me what I already know. Asher is my son!" Stevin yelled angrily; his frustration evident as he whirled around to face Summer.

Summer was taken aback by the anguish in Stevin's eyes. "No, Stevin, that is not at all what I'm saying. This is not an ideal living arrangement for you or me. I know you care for my mom and clearly tolerate my sister, but it must be challenging for you to reside in a household filled with my family members without any privacy. Personally, I cannot continue residing under this roof, knowing everything I'm going through was set in motion by that man. Besides, my reasoning for a blood test is for the Diamonds," Summer said as she gently laid Asher down, walked over to Stevin, embraced him, and rested her head on his chest. He hugged her tightly, planting a kiss on the top of her head.

"I genuinely believe that if I can prove to them that Asher isn't their grandchild, they will leave us alone," she said, tears welling in her eyes. Deep within, Summer harbored a secret motive; no matter how much Asher resembled Stevin, she yearned for absolute certainty. She needed to know for herself that Stevin was undeniably Asher's father.

CHAPTER: 12
TRUE IDENTITY

Stevin emerged from the RV, the warm morning sun casting a golden glow over the bustling truck stop. Exhaustion weighed on him from the long drive; he stretched his arms high above his head intensely, squinting against the light as he spotted his father's robust dually truck. Its polished silver exterior gleamed as it pulled into the lot, the engine's deep rumble resonating like a comforting heartbeat; feeling the air with a sense of familiarity, the sound felt like a welcome melody in his ears.

Just behind him, his cousin Camille trailed in Summer's car. She waved and smiled at him as if he were her favorite person in the world. With a heavy sigh, Stevin took a deep breath, inhaling the mixed aromas of the sharp scent of diesel fuel, mingling with freshly cooked breakfast from the diner, and the faint smell of pine trees from the nearby woods. The sight of his family was a warm embrace, a comforting refuge in the midst of life's chaos.

Stevin had to admit that seeing his family was a sight for sore eyes. The comfort of familiarity swept over him, even though he loved Summer's family dearly; the closeness they shared had started to feel somewhat stifling, like a favorite sweater that had suddenly become too tight.

Understanding the responsibility that lay before him, he felt the weight of his decisions pressing down like a heavy backpack. Life was occurring all around him, chaotic, beautiful, and unpredictable, and he knew this was the life he had chosen, and it was time to face it head-on.

He reached down and adjusted his jeans, a small, determined act that felt symbolic as if he were telling himself to "man up" and pull up his big boy pants and suck it up. This was the life he had embraced when he chose Summer, filled with its trials and tribulations, and he was ready to meet it head on.

Mr. Bash enveloped his son in a warm embrace, pulling him close in a tight hug that felt like a cocoon of safety. For a brief moment, Stevin felt as if his father had magically lifted an enormous weight from his shoulders. It was a moment of profound relief as if he had removed that invisible heavy backpack from his back that was weighing him down, and he immediately shouldered the weight.

"Do you guys have time to sit and have breakfast with me?" Stevin asked, his voice barely above a whisper, tinged with a hint of vulnerability.

"Does bacon come from a pig," Josh chimed in with a booming, hearty laugh that echoed throughout the air. Camile strolled away, releasing her husband's hand as she confidently walked towards the restaurant, her eyes glancing back at Stevin.

"Of course, big cousin! Surely you wouldn't make us drive all this way without treating us all to breakfast," she teased, her playful grin lighting up her face.

"That girl will never change," Stevin chuckled, shaking his head at his father's bemused expression.

"Come on, son," Mr. Bash said, walking behind Stevin and giving his shoulders a reassuring squeeze as if he knew his son needed the motivation.

The playful banter and shared laughter seemed to be just the medicine Stevin needed. His family created an atmosphere of warmth and comfort; the only thing missing was his son and Summer.

The two hours flew by, leaving Stevin feeling like he'd only had ten minutes to enjoy his family's presence. The table was filled with "oohs" and "aahs" as everyone gushed over the countless adorable photos and heartwarming videos of Asher on Stevin's phone. However, as the laughter faded, the air felt thick as a heavy silence began to settle at the table. Camile could sense Stevin's unspoken desire for a moment of alone time with his father.

Camile snatched up the car keys from the table and said, "Come on, Josh. I spotted several boutiques a few miles back. Let's go shopping!"

"Absolutely not, Camile," Josh retorted. "We have a long drive back, and I'm certain your uncle is ready to hit the road. There will be no detours for shopping on this trip," he firmly stated.

"We will just see about that," Camile declared before demanding Josh to let her out of the booth.

"Come on, man!" he exclaimed, looking for support from the guys.

"Son, don't look at me; I don't meddle in marital disputes, especially when it involves a woman and her shopping," Mr. Bash said with a deep chuckle.

Josh glanced over at Stevin, who quickly averted his gaze, not wanting to be involved. Meanwhile, Josh reluctantly followed Camile out of the restaurant, his mind filled with dread of the potential hefty bill she might rack up.

"So, son. How are you doing? You look exhausted," his father said, concern etched on his face.

Stevin hesitated, his gaze dropping to the ground as he let his shoulders droop. He was unwilling to unload the weight of his troubles onto his dad. He didn't want to complicate the already strained relationship with his family regarding Summer and risk worsening it. With a trembling sigh, he cupped his hands over his face as if to create a barrier against his emotions. Silence enveloped them, thick and heavy, while his father's eyes scanned his expression, awaiting an answer.

"Son, look at me," Mr. Bash insisted, his voice firm yet filled with concern.

"Dad, she feels so unreachable," Stevin responded, his voice trembling as he fought back tears. "I've waited and waited for the love of my life to return to me, and all I have is an empty shell of who she once was."

Mr. Bash leaned closer, resting a comforting hand on Stevin's shoulder. "Stevin, you know how much I adore Summer and only want the best for her. But you can't risk saving her, only to lose yourself. You can still be a remarkable friend and an incredible father without losing yourself in this turmoil. I've stood by silently and watched you navigate this storm, giving you the space to make your own choices while offering my support. But I won't stand by and let you drown while trying to pull her from the depths of her darkness.

"I have fellow soldiers who have faced traumas that pale in comparison to what Summer has endured. Yet, their minds have shattered, leaving them ensnared in the dark grip of PTSD, unable to step outside the confines of their homes. They have lost everything — careers, stability, and even the love of their families — rendered unhealable by the horrors they've witnessed.

"You may need to confront the heartbreaking reality that the Summer you once knew may never return and know that this is not your fault. The depths of her experiences are beyond our comprehension. I've delved into her medical reports, and one thing stands clear: that little missy is a true survivor. She possesses a resilience that is nothing short of remarkable; she's one tough cookie. I will give her that."

"Dad, that, I know! One of the most captivating aspects of Summer I was drawn to the most is her sweet innocence and fierce determination to overcome her challenges and survive.

"David has offered to guide us through couple counseling, as well as work with Summer individually, with the goal of helping her to open up and confront the shadows of her past traumas. I know that the woman I love is very much present and wants to love me; she just needs a little more time." Stevin said, sitting up with a glimmer of hope in his eyes.

"Well, son. I'm rooting for both of you. Just promise me one thing: if and when the moment comes to let go, you put yourself and your well-being first," Mr. Bash requested, with a look of concern but also with a strong undercurrent of support, the weight of his words sinking deep into the atmosphere.

"Well, son, shifting gears for a moment. I have some intriguing information you've been eagerly seeking regarding Nate Diamond. Let's make our way to my truck; I've got some detailed files that will shed light on everything. Camile and Josh will be back shortly, and I want to fill you in before they return."

Stevin climbed into the well-worn passenger seat of his dad's truck. The familiar scent of aged leather and lingering tobacco filled the air around him. It enveloped him like a warm embrace, evoking cherished memories of his childhood. He could almost hear his brother's laughter as they rode shotgun next to their father in the driver's seat. The comfort of family and home flooded his mind with memories.

Stevin was jolted back to reality when his father dropped a plain vanilla envelope onto his lap, the name "Nate Schrammer" scrawled across the front in messy handwriting.

"What's this, Dad?" he asked, curiosity lighting up his eyes.

"That my son is a file on Nate Diamond," his father replied, a hint of gravity in his tone. "Nate's great-grandmother was born from an interracial relationship with her German husband, Alexander Schramm. Their family settled in Boston, Massachusetts. Nate's father, Al, was a man struggling to stay afloat in a world that offered little to the poor.

"He worked in a local factory owned by a notorious crime boss, Vinny 'The Butcher' Ferrara, with deep ties to the mob. Ferrara's influence extended far beyond the factory walls, and Al was just a pawn in his dangerous game. Al was tasked with managing the meat locker, a dangerous position that involved facilitating a significant amount of drug trafficking. His extra pay came in the form of a slab of pork that kept food on the table, and his incentive was a shroud of fear. The looming threat of the mob ensured he toed the line, each day a tightrope walk between survival and danger.

"Wait, Dad, this doesn't make sense. The Diamond's net worth is in the millions, and it just doesn't add up."

"Just a moment, son. Give me a chance to finish. When Nate turned fourteen, he began to spiral into rebellion. One night, while out with two of his closest friends, they gave him a gun and, with a mix of challenges, asked, 'Aren't you tired of being poor?'

"Unbeknownst to Nate, the boy's target was Vinny 'The Butcher' Ferrara. Vinny was so confident in his status around town that he was known for moving around solo. Nate's friends had been tracking Vinny for months, studying his every move, and that night sealed Nate Diamond's future, along with his family.

"In a dark alley behind the meat factory, the boys confronted Vinny; both of Nate's friends stood in front of him with guns drawn on Vinny, demanding him in the trunk of his car. Vinny, never blinking, stood firm, staring Nate down as he could see the fear on his face. Nate knew crossing Vinny meant his life and his family life. Without a second thought, he fired two rounds, executing both of his friends with a single bullet to the back of their heads.

"Vinny walked over toward Nate, an imposing figure in the dark alley. With a swift, deliberate motion, he pried the cold metallic gun from the trembling hands of the terrified teenager. The air was thick with tension as Vinny held the weapon firmly, his eyes locked onto Nate's wide, frightened gaze. He stood before him, wiping the gun down and wiping Nate's hand down before placing him in his car. The streetlights flickered overhead as they arrived in front of Nate's run-down apartment complex, casting an eerie glow. Vinny leaned closer, his voice low and intense. "Tonight never happened," he stated firmly, leaving Nate with a chilling sense of uncertainty as the darkness wrapped around them.

"The following morning, Nate heard a firm knock on the door, his heart pounding and body frozen in fear with dread at the sound of Vinny's deep eerie voice. Nate laid awake all night, attempting to process what had occurred, trying to make sense of the horrifying events that had unfolded, the chilling thought of Vinny returning to wreak havoc on his family gnawing at his mind. He curled up in the corner, awaiting the gun shots to begin, when suddenly his bedroom door swung open. His father's presence filled the doorway, startling him. With urgency in his tone, his dad called for him to join the family at the kitchen table, breaking the suffocating silence that had filled the house.

"Nate would learn his fate at that moment. Not only did his unwavering loyalty to Vinny spare his life but the family was instructed to pack up their personal belongings only, as they would be moving into Vinny's high-rise apartments. Al was retired from his position and was never made to work again. Nate, once a scrawny boy jumping off balconies for thrills, now found himself working closely with Vinny. Their operations were eventually shut down by the FBI. While Vinny served fed time, Nate fell off the grid. In his early twenties, he reemerged in California, reinvented as the imposing figure, the man you now know as Nate Diamond! He was untouchable, and his wife, Christopher's mother, mere collateral damage. Nate had a crush on her as a teenager, and once he started working under Vinny, he got what he wanted. Her family married her off to him at the tender age of seventeen. Meanwhile, Vinny remained imprisoned, paradoxically thriving as the wealthiest convict behind bars, his influence still palpable."

Stevin leaned back in disbelief, shock sweeping over him like a sudden storm. "How could Summer get entangled with a family so dangerous?" he pondered, his heart racing. His phone buzzed several times, a string of incoming calls and notifications from Summer, cutting through the haze of his disbelief, but he couldn't answer. His thoughts tumbled chaotically, wrestling with the reality that he had somehow become entwined with the mob. One idea Summer had right was to send the Diamonds a certified blood test result to prove Asher was not one of them, hoping that it would call off the vicious pit bulls.

CHAPTER: 13
UNQUESTIONABLE COMMITMENT

Stevin glances down at his phone, another missed call, accompanied by a text from Summer that read urgent. His mind churned, grappling with the information he had just received about Christopher's father. He needed a moment, just a sliver of time, to gather his thoughts and determine his next move.

As he wrestled with his emotions, resentment bubbled up towards Summer, stinging like an unexpected jab. Her distance towards him, the lack of desire towards him, felt like a sharp thorn in his side, especially since he had sacrificed so much for her. Each day that passed, the burden of his unfulfilled hope, the hope for love that seemed to be slithering away, became heavier, surrounding him like a thick fog that obscured everything else.

He just needed a moment of silence to contemplate his next move without distractions. All the while, his father's stern words also loomed heavily in his mind. Abandoning Summer was not an option; their son was a life tethered to both of them, an unbreakable bond rooted in love and his manly duty. Yet, deep down, he knew he would stand against any force, even if it meant battling Satan himself, to protect his child. There was no room for hesitation; resolution surged within him as he prepared to face whatever came next.

As he swerved the RV onto the gravelly shoulder of the highway, the urgency in Summer's message sent a shiver down his spine. Just as he reached for his phone to dial her back, an incoming call from David lit up the screen.

He's Slipping Away

David and Kimberley entered the home greeted, with a warm embrace from Rose. Kimberley's eyes lit up instantly as Rose planted a loving, wet kiss on her cheek. David's gaze immediately shifted to Summer, who was pacing restlessly in front of the bay window. Rose's eyes widened; meeting David's with a knowing look that silently urged him to step in.

"Hey, baby girl. What's the matter? You look stressed," David said.

"I haven't heard from Stevin since he sent the group text two days ago, saying he had connected the car to the RV and was on his way back. I assumed he might have stopped at a rest area to catch some sleep, but he should have arrived back late last night," Summer replied, anxiety creeping into her voice.

Kimberley chimed in, her brows furrowing in sympathy. "You haven't heard anything from him, sis?"

"Well, I've texted him several times. All my messages show as read, but he hasn't replied back?"

"Let me try calling him," David said as he put the call on speaker.

"Hello, hello!" Stevin answered, his voice booming through the phone."

"Son, are you okay? You had Summer worried. We're just calling to check on you."

"Yes, David. I just pulled over to return Summer's call when you called. My service has been spotty in these mountains, and I'm using my phone for GPS. Tell her I'm 50 miles out; I'll see her in a few. Wait, is everything okay?" Stevin asked, his tone suddenly shifting to concern.

Before David could answer, Summer abruptly stormed out of the room. She had seen Stevin open and read all her texts without replying. In the past, he would never have left her without communicating. Just the mere fact that he never called when he met up with his dad and Camile to Facetime with the baby only reinforced her feeling that her status with his family was null and void, and he was pulling away, leaving her with a deep sense of worry.

A gentle knock at the door pulled Summer out of her deep thoughts. David peeked his head into the bedroom, asking for permission to enter.

"Baby girl, talk to me," he urged, his voice laced with concern.

"I'm losing him, Dad," Summer sobbed, her voice quivering as tears streamed down her cheeks. "And I don't know how to fix it. I don't know how to fix myself."

"What do you mean, Summer? What part of yourself do you feel needs to be fixed? You're the victim here—a brave survivor of a harrowing ordeal. You don't need to be fixed. We, your family, need to understand that you simply need time to process these gruesome events that have occurred to you. Healing begins the moment you accept that I, Summer Teller, was a victim. A victim who has triumphed over her attacker, and now you stand as a survivor. Summer, you can't conquer what you attempt to bury; you must confront, accept, and ultimately heal from the pain."

"David, I'm ready," she whispered. "Please help fix me before I lose him."

"No, Summer," David replied gently but firmly. "I will assist you, guide you, and support you. I won't help you for anyone else's sake, only for you. You must be willing to face these traumatic memories and let go of the blocks you've built. When you find the courage to do that, you will bloom into the best wife, mother, and daughter you can be."

David notices a tiny spark in Summer's dark eyes. "Okay, Dad, I know you're exhausted from your trip. We can revisit this conversation tomorrow."

But David knew it was now or never. He couldn't risk Summer retreating into her emotional shell, disappearing into that familiar darkness that loomed over her.

"No, little missy, you go and check on Asher. Let me wash up, and I'll meet you in the dining room in about 15 minutes."

David hurried up the stairs and informed Rose of what was occurring. He instructed her to take the baby upstairs. He requested that she and Kimberley remain silent and out of sight to create a comfortable environment for Summer, allowing her to feel safe and vulnerable enough to open up.

David returned downstairs to find Summer sitting at the dining room table. She was a portrait of anxiety, her fingers nervously fidgeting with her nails as if she were trying to peel away the layers of her distress. She avoided eye contact, her head bowed low like a wilted flower, unwilling to meet his eyes as the therapy session began.

David took a moment to compose himself before gently guiding her into the session. "Let's start by taking some slow, deliberate breaths," he urged, his voice calm and soothing. "Clear your mind and try to relax."

As Summer began to breathe deeply, the tension in her shoulders seemed to soften. Slowly, she opened up, sharing the tumultuous feelings swirling inside her: an overwhelming sense of disconnection from reality. She described it hauntingly, as if she were submerged in water, her mind drifting back to the day Christopher attempted to drown her while she was pregnant. The vivid memories suffocated her, and the trauma from that day has such a grip on her that she described still tasting the ocean water in her mouth and smelling the dampness that filled her lungs, coupled with the paralyzing fear of closing her eyes in the shower or washing her hair.

Once Summer began to speak and open up, she couldn't stop, detailing some of the most horrific and vulnerable moments she endured at the hands of Christopher.

David, a seasoned psychiatrist with nearly three decades of experience, was deeply shaken by what he heard. Or perhaps the emotional connection he felt toward Summer intensified the impact of her words; she wasn't a mere stranger seeking his counsel, but someone he deeply cared for. The sheer monstrosity of Christopher's actions was unfathomable, leaving David struggling to comprehend how Summer had survived such dire circumstances.

As the session ended, David sat in stunned silence, offering Summer a warm smile as he attempted to maintain his composure, masking the storm of emotions brewing within him. "Take a moment for yourself," he said gently, urging her to bathe and assuring her that he would have Kimberley bring the baby to her shortly.

David waited for Summer to exit the room before he dragged himself from the table, struggling to comprehend what he had just heard. Wanting to keep their session confidential and protect Rose from the horrific truth. Feeling overwhelmed and needing a moment alone, he decided to take a drive but realized his keys were in his jacket pocket upstairs. He entered the bedroom, wanting to avoid Rose at all costs.

"Hey baby, how did it go? Did she open up?" Rose asked.

"Let's talk about it later, Rose. Hey, where's my jacket that was laid across the bed?" David asked, his voice strained as he fought to maintain a facade of calm.

"I hung it up in the closet," Rose answered, moving closer toward David. She could sense something was wrong just by the tone of his voice.

Rose positioned herself in the closet doorway, blocking David from exiting the closet as he refused to look directly at her.

"Rose, not now."

"David, what's wrong," Rose pleaded as she nervously teared up. She gently tugged on David's arm as he pushed past her.

"David, stop!" she shouted.

He halted and turned to face her, tears streaming down his face. Dropping to his knees, he wrapped his arm around Rose's waist, trembling as he cried out. "Rose, it's horrible; what he did to her it's unthinkable."

The commotion drew Kimberley into the bedroom, her concern evident as she saw her father on his knees, distraught, crying while her mother comforted him. Rose signaled for Kimberley to leave and closed the door behind her.

Rose was afraid of what she would hear. Though fear gripped her at the thought of what had affected David so deeply, she knew she had to learn what her baby girl had endured.

CHAPTER: 14
FIGHTING HER WAY BACK

The RV rattled violently as Stevin veered sharply off the main road, the tires crunching loudly over the jagged gravel pavement. He gripped the steering wheel tightly, trying to manage the bulk of the RV, and Summar's car that was hitched to it.

Finally home, the house looming before him. It should have been a comforting site, but it felt far from welcoming. Although he yearned to inhale the sweet scent of his son's soft neck, and to feel the warmth of his tiny body nestled in his arms. Yet, a creeping dread overtook him at the thought of facing Summer. The sting of her rejection haunted him; and he knew he couldn't stomach another cold shoulder from her.

He wrestled with the news he had learned. He knew it was vital to inform David of what he learned. However, he also knew that some truths were better left unspoken, especially for Summer. She was already carrying so much on her shoulders that there was no need to add to her fears. So he decided to keep the weight of that knowledge to himself, hoping to shield her from further concerns.

Stevin, feeling fatigued and in need of a hot meal and shower, decided to unhitch the travel trailer to avoid having to do any manual labor the following day. He looked and saw Kimberley leaping from the porch and walking towards him. Not really in the mood for small talk, he sucked up his feelings and gave a polite smile.

"What's going on, Kimberley?"

"Stevin, I know you are tired, but you might want to go check on Summer."

"I intend to do so, right after I unhook her car. I know she's upset she was unable to reach me. Your mom called earlier and gave me an earful."

"I wish it was that simple. At Summer's request, Dad counseled her, and I can only say that whatever she shared with my dad broke him. I heard some commotion coming from my parent's bedroom; I walked in to find my father on his knees, broken down in tears, with my mom comforting him. He kept repeating, 'It's bad, Rose; what he did to her is unthinkable."

"Where is Summer now?" Stevin asks, his expression full of concern.

"I haven't seen her. Their session ended about twenty minutes ago. Asher is currently napping in the nursery."

As Stevin started to walk away, Kimberley gently grabbed him by the arm. "I'm sorry, Stevin, for everything. You might want to speak with Dad first before you see Summer so you can know what you're about to walk into. Don't worry about your belongings in the RV. I will clean up out here and bring everything in."

Stevin softly stepped into the house, making his first stop at Asher's Nursery. He was eager to lay eyes on his little guy as he gently pushed the door open. To his surprise, Summer was standing over Asher's crib, running her fingers through his soft, curly hair. Surprisingly, Summer appeared calm; she didn't seem upset at all. He decided it was best not to mention what Kimberley had shared with him. Their gaze met, and her lips curved into a half-smile.

"Hello, sweetheart. You both are a sight for sore eyes," he said warmly, moving closer. He walked behind Summer, his touch tender as he rubbed her shoulders while admiring their son. As he leaned in to kiss her forehead, she surprised him by swiftly rising onto her tiptoes, capturing his lips in a soft, unexpected kiss. For a heartbeat, time seemed to pause as he stood there, his eyes closed, feeling a delightful shiver down his spine from her soft lips. The serenity was short-lived when she softly spoke and asked if they could talk.

"Yes, darling, we can talk," he replied, his heart racing as blood rushed to his third leg.

"How about you feed your son first? It's time for his feeding," she suggested, handing him a warm bottle. "I'll fix you a dinner plate, and afterward, you can shower. Then we can talk."

Settling into the rocking chair with Asher cradled in his arms. Stevin stared into his son's eyes as he eagerly consumed the four-ounce bottle, finishing every drop before he was relieved of burping duty as Summer informed him his dinner plate was ready.

Stevin quickly scoffed down his dinner, eager to talk to David and gain insight into what Summer had shared with him. As he watched Summer enter the nursery to change Asher's dirty diaper, he spun on his heels and dashed up the stairs.

He approached Rose's and David's bedroom door and gently tapped against it, but it cracked open, revealing Rose, her eyes red and swollen from tears. She eased out the door quietly, shutting the door softly behind her.

Grasping Stevin's hand, she leads him across the hall into Kimberley's room.

"Hey, Mom. I wanted to talk with David regarding Summer."

Rose silently shook her head no. "No, son. Just let him sleep," she said, her voice trembling. Suddenly, tears streamed down her cheeks as she pressed her hands against Stevin's chest. "Son, we need to give her time; we must protect her at all costs. He tried to drown my baby," she cried out, leaning into him, her head resting against his chest as her sobs shook her small frame. "That monster pulled her into the ocean and tried to drown her. She needs us, son; she needs you. She needs your patience and understanding, Stevin."

The weight of Rose's words hung in the air, a stark reminder of the battle they were facing. Summer had previously revealed the chilling truth about Christopher: his cold-hearted nature and the monster that lurked beneath his charming facade. With every word Rose spoke, Stevin felt an unsettling familiarity; nothing shocked him anymore when it came to the that despicable SOB.

Yet, amidst the chaos, the most critical task at hand was to remain calm for Summer. For the first time since her return, she had shown him some affection; it felt as if she was finally willing to peel back the layers of pain and vulnerability to let him in. Stevin knew he had to put his anger and emotions on the back burner, prioritizing her peace.

Before stepping into the shower, he made a quick trip to the RV, locating his hidden bottle of cognac he had stashed away. He uncorked it and tipped the bottle, feeling the rich warmth liquor slide down his throat, momentarily quenching the unquenchable thirst that mirrored his anxiety. With a heavy sigh, he returned to the house, ready to wash away the day's tensions.

Summer noticed that Stevin had showered in the ensuite bathroom connected to their bedroom instead of the one upstairs, which had been his usual choice. As she approached the bed, preparing to settle down, the bathroom door suddenly swung open. She was facing the door, almost as if she were anticipating him opening it. Her gaze fixed on him, a scene that felt too familiar. He stepped into view, steam swirling around him like a veil, showcasing his impressive physique. His masculine body was fully on display. His skin glistened with droplets of water, and the air was thick with his shower's warm, fragrant scent.

She couldn't tear her eyes away, feeling a whirlwind of emotions crashing within her; hell, she was damaged, but not dead. Waves of emotions surged within her, flooding her every thought and overwhelming her with the vividness of feelings she believed were lost forever.

With a heavy heart, Summer quickly dropped her head, the weight of uncertainty pulling her down as she sank onto the edge of the bed. The last thing she wanted was to awaken the restless beast within Stevin, a desire she feared she couldn't fully satisfy. At that moment, she was caught in a delicate balancing act, striving to mend their fragile relationship instead of driving him further away.

Unbeknownst to her, Stevin was intoxicated, and the kiss they had shared earlier had awakened the beast he had attempted to keep tamed. When he emerged nude, he noticed her knees trembling beneath her, which only intensified his desire, realizing he still had that effect on her. At that moment, talking was the furthest thing from his mind.

Summer took a hard swallow, her heart racing, as she stared wide-eyed at Stevin as he walked directly towards her, failing to get dressed. He halted just inches before her, his body rock hard and still, as if he were inviting her to bridge the gap and make the first move.

When she failed to engage, he gently lifted her to her feet, his arms enveloping her in a warm embrace. He anticipated the softness of her body melting into his arms, a comforting connection that never came. But instead, her body was stiff and rigid. He released her, and she plopped back down onto the bed.

"You really hate me. Do I disgust you?" he asked, disbelief flickering across his face. The oppressive silence that followed only magnified his uncertainty. He lingered only for a few seconds, which felt like an eternity to him before he turned to walk away.

"No, Stevin. Please don't go," she pleaded, her fingers gripping his arms with a surprising strength, desperation lacing her voice.

He whirled around to confront her, his eyes blazing with frustration.

"What do you want from me, damn it? I'm standing right here; I've always been right here." His voice raised with mounting intensity. "I don't know what you want from me, Summer. Why can't you tell me what you need from me? When you look at me, who do you really see? I'm not CHRISTOPHER!"

Once again, silence filled the room before he abruptly snatched away. Summer jumped to her feet, her heart racing, and declared, "I see nothing; I see nothing when I look at you."

The expression in Stevin's eyes darkened, shifting from deep sadness to simmering anger. Fed up with the conversation, he stormed into the bathroom to get dressed. Summer quickly followed and positioned herself in front of the door, blocking his escape.

"Do you love me, Stevin?"

"What type of fuckin question is that? Are you seriously questioning my loyalty?" he shot back, his voice tinged with disbelief and hurt.

"Not at all! I'm just trying to get your attention. I need for you to stop and hear me."

"What, Summer? I'm right here, and yet you feel a million miles away."

Summer turned and walked away. Her thoughts were jumbled, and her words wouldn't form correctly. She sat back on the edge of the bed, her upper body falling back against the mattress, and began to wail. Stevin straggled himself on top of her, his body radiating heat and his breaths coming in harsh, deep burst as he demanded her attention. He took her feet and gently pushed her entire body into the bed.

"Tell me, baby, what do you see when you see me?

"I see crashing waves. For months, my cries were swallowed by the roaring thundering waves, till eventually, the chaotic rhythm of the waves transformed from a source of torment into a strange distraction. The sound was so overpowering that it seemed to consume all my anguish.

"I got so deeply lost in the rhythmic lullaby that it drowned out my inner turmoil to block out when he forced himself on me until I couldn't get out of that trance. I'm finding it difficult to dissociate forced intimacy from love and it being a conscious choice. When your fingers brush against my skin, it's like an out-of-body experience. It feels like I've transcended reality; my mind is swept away by a relentless tide of crashing waves, each surge echoing memories of Christopher. For so long, this has been my refuge, my coping mechanism, and now I feel lost, unsure of how to escape my own thoughts."

Stevin sat up in bed, a determined gaze in his eyes. "Summer, do you trust me"? She slowly nodded her head, yes. "No, Summer, I need to hear it part from your lips. Do you trust me?"

With a deep breath, Summer met his gaze and replied, "Yes, Stevin. I trust you wholeheartedly with my life." Her voice was strong, filled with a conviction that resonated in the air between them.

"I need you to close your eyes," he said. Without hesitation, Summer complied with his request.

"Who am I?" he murmured softly, pressing a tender kiss to her forehead, his breath warm against her skin. Summer, caught off guard by his question, opened her eyes and turned her head slightly to look at him.

"No, Summer, close your eyes," Stevin gently insisted, his fingers cradling her chin to guide her head back to its original position. She complied and closed her eyes. "Now, say my name," he implored, his voice filled with an intensity that sent shivers down her spine.

"Stevin," she breathed, her voice barely above a whisper.

"Again," he encouraged, his tone soothing to her ears.

"Stevin Bash," she replied, drawing a deep, steady breath that seemed to electrify the air around them with an unspoken intimacy.

As he tenderly touched her body. He guided her to keep her eyes closed while she repeated his name as he tenderly kissed her lips, his warmed tongue softly sucking her fingers. Every gentle touch made her heart race with anticipation.

He watched as her body quivered as he fully undressed her, and she lay vulnerable to his command. He didn't have to request for her to repeat his name as she began to repeat it with every touch, never opening her eyes.

As he traced his hand from her stomach up to her cleavage, she surrendered to his touch, her breath growing deeper with each caress, welcoming his advances.

Demanding she keep saying his name. He sat up on his knees, watching her respond to his touch. He easily guided her legs apart, straddling them, giving himself a clear eye view of her throbbing, moist lips. Running his tongue along her folds in long strokes before his tongue brushed against her clit, silence consumed her as her legs locked around his head. Not giving her a chance to reject him, he quickly shifted his body upwards for a wet, passionate kiss while sliding his throbbing manhood into her tight, pulsating muscles.

Summer sucked in the air and squeezed her eyes shut. The kiss of his warm mouth cupped hers, his tongue deep and hot. Stevin attempted to control his strokes as her muscles clenched tight around his shaft, gripping as she clenched and unclenched his throbbing cock.

Wrapping his arms around her, he held her tightly, slowing down his strokes as he savored the feel of her wet juices splashing against him with each stroke. Summer, fully aware of her reality as she stares deep into Stevin's eyes, her entire body shook with intensity. She bit her lip to keep quiet and muffled her moans as Stevin's strokes became harder and deeper. She could feel him swell with each hard thrust, his moans intensifying her orgasm as she moaned out his name. Her moans drove him mad as she could fill his throbbing manhood swelling inside her before he let out a loud moan, and his cock felt like a throbbing pulse as he released his built-up pressure inside her, demanding her to say his name!

CHAPTER: 15
HIS DARK SECRET

Stevin and Summer's connection was short-lived; she quickly retreated back into her shell, creating distance between them. Before the steam of their steamy intimate moment could dissipate, Summer had slowly inched away from Stevin, moving to the edge of the bed. He recognized that she needed time to adjust to sharing the same bed again.

However, when she ultimately decided to leave the bed entirely and curled up in the recliner, a wave of anger washed over him.

Frustrated by her choice, he awakened her from her sleep, his voice tinged with irritation as he said, "The bed is all yours."

Consequently, he found himself restless, tossing and turning on the uncomfortable daybed located in Asher's nursery.

Like a crowing rooster heralding the dawn, Summer's eyes fluttered open like an alarm clock. A deep ache for Stevin's presence settled in her chest as she awaited his entrance into the bedroom to cradle their son before his feeding. Blinking away the sleep from her eyes, she noticed Asher's bassinet- a familiar sight and source of comfort- was missing from its usual corner, and Stevin was nowhere in sight.

A sense of unease filled her as she recalled how her and Stevin's night ended. She slowly crossed the home, the floorboards creaking softly beneath her feet. When she reached the nursery door and gently pushed it open, peeping inside. Her heart sank at the sight of Stevin sprawled out on the daybed, one leg hanging limply over the edge, and Asher's crib empty.

Summer turned and made her way upstairs to locate her baby. When she reached the top of the stairs, she noticed that Rose's bedroom door was slightly ajar. She tiptoed into the room and approached Asher's bassinet. There, nestled cozily, was Asher tossing his head back and forth, his little face a picture of impatience, clearly signaling that breakfast was long overdue. She gently picked him up and headed back downstairs to the nursery.

Stevin was startled awake by the shifting of the mattress as Summer sat down near his head. His eyes popped open, and to his surprise, he was met with the soft brush of her lips against his.

"Please make today your last day sleeping on this back-buster mattress, Stevin."

A frown creased his brow. "That's not the energy you had last night. You couldn't get me out of your bed fast enough."

"That's simply not true, Stevin. First of all, you wore me out; I barely had the strength to string two coherent words together by the time we finally settled down. And secondly, my anxiety attacks are unbearable, especially when it's hot." Summer's tone shifted slightly, a hint of vulnerability creeping in. She refrained from sharing the darker memories that haunted her, causing triggered flashbacks to when she had been chained to a metal frame headboard in the scorching heat for days.

"I feel as if I'm suffocating. Mom doesn't help the situation; she insists keeping the house warm is for Asher's benefit, but honestly, I think she's just cold-natured. She refuses to let me lower the thermostat at night. I eased out of bed to prevent from disturbing you."

"Summer, you were on the edge of the bed before you decided to get up completely."

"Yes, Stevin. I tossed and turned throughout the night; your body heat made me even hotter. I was attempting not to wake you. That was all! I eased open the window, letting a cool breeze flow in, and pulled the recliner close to it, and I was out of it. I recall you waking me, but I was simply too drained to respond. I want you in our bed, right next to me. But my anxiety is real. I can't help it."

"Perhaps David can order you something that will ease your anxiety and help you sleep," Stevin suggested, glancing over at her with concern. "I'll go wash up while you finish feeding him."

A satisfied grin spread across his face as he admired Summer and their son while she nursed him. "Look at him, slurping away as if it's the best thing he's ever tasted! That's right, Daddy's little man," he said, leaning in, kissing Asher on the cheek as he whispered. "So that you know, these melons belong to Papa. You got eight months and these titties coming back home to big daddy! Besides I had enough of your milk last night. So much that daddy doesn't even need to add milk to my cereals this morning," he teased.

Summer's mouth fell open in surprise as she hurled a pillow at Stevin's head. She had forgotten for a brief moment about his unfiltered sense of humor. A quirky charm that always managed to catch her off guard.

The family was surprised when they all came downstairs, drawn by the delightful aroma of breakfast spilling throughout the air. The crisp scent of sizzling bacon mingled with the sweet smell of freshly baked pancakes, creating an irresistible symphony of fragrances that beckoned them into the kitchen. David, however, felt particularly unsettled. He had tossed and turned all night, struggling to process Summer's startling revelation, and now, the sight that greeted him was surreal. Yet here she is, in the kitchen, smiling and preparing breakfast for the family.

Typically, David maintained a strictly professional demeanor with his clients and did not push a Q&A session outside their therapy session, but he felt compelled to understand how she was truly doing.

David waited until Summer moved towards the sink, creating some distance from everyone else. He then eased up behind her, placing his hand on her upper back and asking, "Baby girl, are you okay?"

Summer turned to him, his expression clouded with confusion. "David, it's okay; we can talk in front of everyone," she assured him.

Summer then asked everyone to grab their plates and take a seat at the table so she could speak with them. Before she could begin, Stevin jumped in, his voice cutting through the air, asking David about a safe prescription option for her anxiety. David wanted the conversation about medication to be led by Summer, so he simply replied that he would address options with both of them later in a counseling session.

Summer promptly interjected, informing both David and Stevin that she preferred to continue solo therapy sessions with David before starting couples therapy with Stevin. She reached out to clasp Stevin's hand, her eyes searching for his understanding, worried about his reaction. Stevin nodded in agreement, a calm acceptance in his demeanor. The one session she had had with David had already begun to peel back layers of her emotion, which helped her open up some.

David immediately shut down the conversation, urging Summer if she felt she needed to address the family to do it individually, knowing some topics were far easier to navigate on a one-on-one basis. Wanting Summer to open up in her own time, free from the burden of trying to satisfy anyone else's expectations.

Rose interjected with a hint of impatience, "No, David. If she wants to speak with us, let's allow her the space to do so." Not fully understanding the sensitive nature of Summer's situation, she lacked awareness of the delicate balance required to support her. David recognized that Summer's raw feelings and past traumas needed to be addressed in carefully measured steps.

He was consumed with worry about the fragile bond between Summer and Kimberley, a relationship that could fall apart at any moment. He realized that Summer hadn't had the opportunity to fully grasp the impact of Kimberley's actions on her life nor to confront the profound role she played in her recent traumas. A looming, difficult conversation awaited the sisters, one that held the weight of unspoken emotions and unresolved feelings. He dreaded the thought of Summer being pushed into a premature forgiveness without first being able to voice her pain and truly grapple with her feelings towards her sister. The tension in their relationship hung in the air like a storm, and he hoped for a moment of clarity that would allow both of them to find peace.

"Mom, listen to Dad," Kimberley chimed in, her voice slightly rising. "He is the professional here; he knows what's best for her. I see a difference in her mood; she seems much lighter. Either Dad is damn good at what he does, are Stevin is even better," she teased, her eyes flickering toward Summer as she cast a playful wink at her. "I notice Asher stayed in Mom's room last night."

"Dammit, Kimberley, learn how to read the room!" David shouted, his voice escalating to a startled shout that echoed through the dining area. The sudden outburst jolted Asher awake from his peaceful nap, setting off a chain reaction as each family member began to rise from the table, one by one, discomfort etched on their faces.

"What did I say? It was just a joke!" Kimberley blurted out, her voice mix of confusion and frustration as she watched her family disperse.

Stevin approached David with a serious look, informing him he had some information he needed to share that needed to be kept between them. He also mentioned Summer's discomfort with being out in public and expressed the need to pick up some items for the baby, including a portable air conditioner. Stevin was determined to make Summer comfortable and sought out a solution to keep them in the same bed.

David offered to drive to the local department store, where the two of them shop for the household, even lucking up and finding a small portable AC unit.

They stopped at a local diner so Stevin could update David on the information he learned regarding the Diamond's background and their connection with the mob. Stevin's energy shifted quickly; a dark cloud seemed to hang over him as he asked David for some alone time. He mentioned that the diner was less than five miles from their house, so he would walk back home.

David urged Stevin to reconsider, fearing that once he left, Stevin would turn to the bar as his coping mechanism. He felt a heavy weight in his chest as he contemplated the need to share Stevin's secret with Summer. The idea of placing another burden on her overwhelmed him, yet he knew her support could be crucial in confronting Stevin's struggle with alcohol.

As David drove into the driveway, he spotted the women taking a leisurely stroll. A gentle smile gracing Summer's face as she pushed Asher in his stroller. The warm breeze rustled the leaves, a refreshing change from the chilly weather they had experienced since moving there. Determined to give them some space, he unloaded the bags from the car and stayed out of sight.

As the balmy breeze blew against her face, Summer felt a rush of exhilaration surge through her body. The fresh air filled her lungs, replacing the fog of anxiety that typically clouded her thoughts. The stroll with the family and the chance to escape the confining walls of her new, forced home was precisely what she needed.

However, that fleeting sense of liberation quickly shattered when they approached a hauntingly familiar cliff. A wave of déjà vu washed over her, sending a chill spiraling down her spine, prickling the hairs on the back of her neck. The eerie sight was a vivid reminder of her recurring nightmare. The sight before her was a steep drop-off, with fast-moving river water swirling over a shallow, rocky bottom. Time seemed to freeze as fear gripped her heart, leaving her immobile.

Noticing Summer's grip on the stroller handle and the fear in her eyes. Rose placed a comforting hand on Summer's trembling hand. "Baby girl, what's the matter," Rose asked, her voice filled with concern.

"Mom, a couple of years ago, I had this constant nightmare of Christopher chasing me. It's dark, and there's snow everywhere. I'm running and running until I reach this very ledge, and then I fall to my death."

Before Rose or Kimberley could collect their thoughts to respond to Summer's shocking revelation, a sudden presence startled them all. Summer instinctively flinched, her heart pounding as she clutched the stroller tightly, teetering on the edge of running away.

Stevin had spotted the mother-daughter duo on his walk home and decided to quicken his pace to catch up with them. He followed behind in silence, not alerting them of his presence until he was right behind them. Suddenly, playfully grabbing Summer by her waist, slurring in his tipsy stupor, "Where are you guys headed?"

Summer was extremely upset that Stevin could be so insensitive to her situation, especially knowing her state of mind. Shifting the stroller toward home, she quickly walked away.

Rose could smell the liquor on Stevin, so when he attempted to follow after Summer, she swiftly grabbed him by the arm, gave him an unapproving look, and said, "No," forbidding him to go after her before walking away, leaving him soaking in his feelings.

Kimberley stood in silence, staring at him before walking away. Suddenly, she turned around and said, "You know, bro, you're too intelligent to be acting like a box of rocks." The sting of her words lingered in the air as she walked away, leaving him standing alone on the deserted path, feeling the sharp bite of isolation.

Summer arrived at the house first, and David could immediately tell something was wrong. Before he could grasp the situation, Rose and Kimberley stumbled through the door, their faces etched with concern as they rushed to comfort Summer. Gently, she unfastened Asher from the stroller, her hands trembling slightly as she did so. It didn't take long for David to figure out what had happened, and in that moment, his main concern was for Stevin.

Before going to search for Stevin to ensure he was okay, David delivered the heavy news to Summer that Stevin had turned to alcohol to cope with her disappearance. He urged the women to withhold judgment, emphasizing the importance of offering support.

"As a man, there are some burdens we carry in silence, sharing only what is necessary to shield you from the weight of it all. There are countless things you ladies are not privy to and believe me when I say Stevin is shouldering a tremendous load. If you want to help him break free from the grip of the bottle, wrap him in your compassion, your love, and your understanding," David said, his eyes reflecting the deep empathy he felt for Stevin and his situation.

CHAPTER: 16
HIS TERM'S

Summer sat on the sofa, absorbing the information that David had shared. She was fully aware that Stevin had sacrificed a great deal on her behalf. After the initial shock had subsided and she was away from the eerie sight of the cliff, she realized that she might have reacted too harshly towards him in front of everyone.

David stepped through the doorway first, followed by Stevin, who shuffled past everyone with his head down, shutting himself up in the bedroom.

The pep talk from David was greatly appreciated, and although David lifted him up, the hurt and embarrassment were too overwhelming for him to face the others.

Summer carefully placed Asher into Rose's arms and followed Stevin into the bedroom. The atmosphere was heavy with unspoken words as she sat on the edge of the bed, her eyes locked onto Stevin. Tears could be seen falling from the corner of his eyes; he turned his head, avoiding having to face her. The soft hum of the portable AC that Stevin had purchased for her caught her attention, intensifying the deep ache for him, as each tear he shed spoke volumes of the pain he was trying to mask.

David had managed to set up the small portable unit in the bedroom while they were out for their walk.

Feeling a surge to shower him with affection, Summer straddled herself on top of Stevin, positioning herself so their faces were mere inches apart. She tenderly pressed small, lingering kisses against his lips, tracing the contours of his face and planting gentle pecks on his hands.

"You are perfect," she whispered, her voice a soothing melody as she pressed her lips to his skin, planting soft kisses in a tender rhythm. "You are my protector, my husband, my best friend. My life would be incomplete without you, baby," she confessed, her eyes sparkling with sincerity. She wrapped her arms around him, feeling the heat of his body against hers while her fingers gently caressed the back of his neck as she hummed their favorite song in his ear.

Although Stevin didn't verbally acknowledge her affection towards him, he closed his eyes and surrendered to the warmth of her love. He longed to feel accepted and appreciated, and her nurturing touch, along with her soothing words, washed away the cloud of doubt that had lingered in his mind. All he desired was to remain cocooned in her embrace.

Just as he began to lose himself in the tranquility of her affection, a soft knock on the bedroom door interrupted the serene silence. Summer lifted her head with curiosity, granting permission for the person outside the door to enter.

Rose entered the room, "Summer, could you give me a moment along with my son."

Summer slowly removed herself from the bed and exited the room. Stevin, however, avoided making eye contact with Rose.

"Son, please sit up and look at me," Rose requested gently.

Stevin propped himself up, his face a canvas of sorrow, as if he had just lost his dearest friend. Rose's heart ached as she could see he had been crying. "Stevin, when your mother had to discipline you verbally when you were younger, did you ever question her love for you?"

Stevin shook his head no in response.

"Then, my son, never question mine," she continued, her voice firm yet tender. "I know who you are and what you mean to my daughter and our family. I will forever be indebted to you and grateful for you. My daughter is alive because of you; she is whole because of you, and our family is together because of you. You are forever a part of our family.

"I might never know the burdens you bear to keep Summer safe and our family united, but I'm deeply grateful for you. As a family, we stand together as your support system; you have eight shoulders to lean on- please use them."

With a soft kiss on his forehead, she lingered for a moment, letting her warmth envelop him before she turned to walk out the door, leaving him with her love and unwavering support.

Summer sat on the sofa, fidgeting like a nervous school-aged girl, her mind racing with worry about what her mom was saying to Stevin. When she heard her bedroom door open, she looked up to see Rose walking towards her. "Baby girl, we're heading to the diner for dinner. We'll bring you both something back. I'll have Kimberley text you the menu."

Summer nodded and promptly returned to her bedroom, with Asher cradled in her arms. As she entered the room, she found Stevin sitting on the edge of the bed. She gently swaddled Asher and placed him in the bassinet. Summer could feel Stevin's warmth as he stood behind her, his eyes fixed on Asher. With a swift motion, he lifted her and carried her to the bed, wrapping himself around her as they lay in silence, eventually drifting off to sleep.

Summer was awakened by the soft cries of her son and the constant buzzing of her cell phone, which was vibrating non-stop from Kimberley's calls, attempting to get their dinner order.

As Summer attended to Asher's needs, Stevin ended a call with Rose, informing her that he and Summer would just take a burger and fries for dinner. Summer settled into the recliner, nursing their son, as she stared at Stevin from across the room. She could sense that something was troubling him.

Stevin waited until she had burped Asher and returned to his side before dropping the bombshell.

He spoke, and Summer's heart sank in her stomach. "Summer, Asher is scheduled for his six-week checkup next week. I will wait a few days after his immunization, and then I will be traveling alone with him to my parent's home for a week.

"Stevin, no!" Summer cried out, snatching away from him.

"Summer, please don't take this personally as an attack on you. Right now, I desperately need the presence of my parents, and it's only fair they get to meet their grandson in person."

"Why can't they come here, Stevin?" Summer retorted, her eyes wide with disbelief. "The fact that you're trying to separate me from my son is absolutely ludicrous."

"They can't come here for the same reason you can't go there," he reasoned. "The tensions are too high between you and my family. I need time to mend you guys relationship. And honestly, I miss my family. All I'm asking is for a short visit; I would like my parents to have a chance to enjoy their grandson, the same opportunity your family gets daily. I understand your concerns, which I will address them to ensure you are completely comfortable with the travel arrangements. But, what I can't understand is if you give me pushback on my son meeting my parents, baby."

"That's not at all the issue, Stevin! How do you expect to drive and tend to an infant at the same time? You are asking me to be okay with you, the love of my life, and my child being put in direct danger."

"I'm going to have someone drive us a state over, and then we'll fly out just like David and your sister travel. I'll work out the travel logistics with Orlando connections, and you can supply me with enough milk for the trip. I promise I won't leave my parent's farm, and I can assure you our son will be protected at all times."

Summer sat in stunned silence, crying and shaking her head. "How could he?" she thought bitterly.

***

Stevin knew he needed David on his side, getting him onboard as he included him in the security measures and informing him about the private investigators his father had hired to trail Christopher and his father. The duo was being kept under close watch, ensuring that they remained in Los Angeles during his travels. However, the atmosphere among the women was tense, and their disapproval of Stevin's decision was evident.

Days passed with Summer barely acknowledging him, her silent plea for him to reconsider. Yet, in the end, Stevin wasn't taking no for an answer. Eventually, Summer finally agreed after speaking with Mr. Bash and Orlando, who ensured that every security detail was handled. Providing her with some sense of security. They reassured her that if anything slightly suspicious occurred, Mr. Bash would personally escort Stevin and the baby home along with the detailed security they had hired around the farm.

Stevin gazed intently at Summer as she sat on the edge of the bed, her hands trembling while she struggled to secure Asher into his car seat. Her beautiful, big, sad brown eyes filled with tears of sorrow. When their gazes met, he could see the piercing sting of disdain reflected in her eyes. He couldn't blame her for being upset; he just needed her to trust him as her lover, best friend, and the father of their child.

Stepping closer, he wrapped his arms gently around her waist, urging her to face him. His touch was tender, his fingers light as they softly grasped her chin, turning her towards him.

"Summer, I'm not asking you to ignore your worries or pretend everything is okay, but I need you to trust me. Please, give me this chance; hell, give my family this opportunity to enjoy their son and grandson."

"Yeah, and in the process, this 'happy family reunion' of yours can shatter every safe space you and my family have created for me and your son. What's the point of hiding out in these mountains if you're willing to risk it all because you're swept up in your emotions?"

Stevin turned away, his shoulders slumping as he sank onto the bed. Her words hit him like a punch to the gut, leaving him breathless, as though she had stolen the air from his lungs.

Heck, who was he fooling? He knew Summer was right; he just wasn't willing to allow the Diamonds to come between his parents and their grandson.

Although her heart ached at the sight of him feeling conflicted, she wasn't willing to pretend his decision for their family wasn't reckless.

Stevin's cell phone dinged, breaking the silence in the room. Rose's dad had volunteered to drive Stevin 200 miles to another state, where he would purchase their flight tickets upon arrival. He had been scouting for airline tickets that would align with the departure time he needed.

He leaned over and kissed Summer on the forehead, then took a tight grip on Asher's car seat, grabbed his luggage, and walked out of the bedroom.

As Stevin rushed out of the door, David quickly grabbed Rose and shut her inside their bedroom. She was furious with Summer for agreeing to put her son in harm's way and even angrier with Stevin.

The bitter reality that no one had taken her feelings into consideration when inviting her father around intensified her irritation. He was the architect of this chaos; it was he who put all this in motion when he decided to rip Summer away from her. In a fiery outburst, she expressed her frustration loudly; the walls weren't thick enough to contain her fury. Stevin caught the brunt of her harsh words but continued to walk out the door.

In the stillness that followed, Summer stood frozen in silence. Guilt gnawed at her, leaving her feeling torn and disappointed in herself for letting her mom down. Meanwhile, Rose, fueled by her emotions, pushed past David; she needed to look Stevin in his eyes so he could see how disappointed she was with him. But instead, she found herself staring into Summer's sorrowful eyes.

Overwhelmed by the whirlwind of emotions, Rose immediately stormed back into the bedroom, followed closely by David, his frustration bubbling to the surface. He didn't hold back as he confronted her, his voice raised with anger.

"What has gotten into you, Rose? Are you satisfied now? Did you see the pain on your daughter's face? Look, I get it; we are all exhausted. I'm headed back home in a couple of days, and this situation has taken a toll on us all. I think it's a good idea for Kimberley to stay, and you should take a break and come home with me."

With a defiant pull away, Rose shot back, "I'm not leaving my child, David!"

"Rose, I can only do so many teleconferences with my patients. I have to return every six weeks for in-home evaluations, and for this to work, I also need my wife by my side. Darling, you do understand that this is only temporary for both of us. We will guarantee Summer and Stevin have what they need, but we also have our lives to return to."

Rose knew in her heart David was right, but she was too stubborn to acknowledge it at the time. Instead, she retreated downstairs to Summer's bedroom.

When Summer heard her bedroom door squeal open, she lifted her head and met Rose's gaze. She felt too drained to talk and too emotional to explain her decision. With a shuddering sigh, she buried her tear-streaked face back into the softness of her pillow as she stared blankly at her phone.

Stevin had FaceTime her with the camera focused on Asher and the volume muted. Rose curled up behind Summer; her mother's comforting presence against the moment's heaviness helped her relax. Together, they watched intently as Asher, with his wide, curious eyes, gradually closed as he drifted to sleep.

Timed seemed to slow as Summer remained on the call until it was time for Stevin to board the plane. Finally, exhaustion overcame her, and she closed her eyes for a nap, setting her alarm clock to wake her at the time their flight was scheduled to land.

***

Stevin kept his promise by including Summer as much as possible during his stay. However, tensions remained high, mainly because none of the older women, particularly Mrs. Irene, would acknowledge her. Summer's small, desperate voice echoed through the phone as she tried to include herself in the conversations pertaining to Asher.

Stevin had expressed his displeasure to his mom about how she had been treating Summer, as she did everything to make Summer uncomfortable on calls. Mr. Bash, typically a voice of reason, remained silent, not intervening in the conflict. Feeling hurt, Summer's wall went up, and she stopped attempting to speak, only giving her attention to her son. Despite the uncomfortable situation, she couldn't deny seeing the Bash's cuddling over Asher and bonding with him melted her heart. It was a kind of love she had only dreamed of receiving as a child, and now she saw her son receiving it.

Finally, Stevin was acting like the man she had fallen in love with. He was confident and happy in the moments he spent on the farm.

Rose observed the situation from a distance with growing displeasure, particularly toward Mrs. Irene, often rolling her eyes in frustration. She made it clear to her daughter that she should never allow anyone to make her feel unwelcome. "If they want to be part of Asher's life, they must accept you as his mom. If not, they can go to hell! I refuse to stand by and watch anyone make you feel less than!"

Summer smiled and hugged Rose, cherishing their bonding time alone. However, their moment was interrupted by a call from Kimberley begging Summer to step away from Rose so she could speak with her privately.

Summer stepped away and walked into the bedroom. "What's going on, Kimberley?"

"Summer, can you please come and get me. Don't tell Mom. I just need someone to talk to. I can't face mom right now."

"Where are you? Summer asked, her curiosity piqued."

"I'm at the airport."

"You flew directly in? Summer's voice escalated, laced with anxiety.

"No, I have not compromised you. Papa Joe rented me a car in his name. The airport is my drop-off location, sis; please, Kimberley pleaded, desperation creeping into her words."

Summer took a few deep breaths, feeling very uncomfortable about lying to Rose. She yelled from downstairs, "Mom, I'll be right back," and quickly dashed out the door before any questions could be asked.

Summer slowly circled the parking lot, scanning for Kimberley when she suddenly dashed out from behind a parked car. She opened the passenger door and plopped down in the seat. Her face was swollen, her eyes were puffy, and her shoulders trembled as she buried her face in her hands.

"I don't know what I did in my past life to deserve such a screwed-up life in this one!" she cried out, her voice breaking with despair.

Summer, who had always been detached from her own emotions and typically the person in need of support, was at a loss. Usually, on the receiving end of support, she had never been in a position where she needed to provide it. Feeling uncomfortable and an unfamiliar tightness in her chest, she mustered the courage to lean closer, placing her hand on Kimberley's shoulder.

"What's wrong, Kimberley?" she asked, feeling utterly unprepared to offer comfort, not knowing how she would be much help. She knew she couldn't ignore her sister's pain, especially since Kimberley looked as if she were heartbroken.

"Last year, while traveling back and forth, I met this guy named Max. I wasn't looking to meet anyone, Summer, but he was so kind and provided a welcome distraction from everything I had been going through with you and our parents. Our encounter happened unexpectedly while I was on the road; he was sweet enough to help me when I got a flat tire.

"Sis, I've been traveling back and forth just to see Max. My parents are under the impression that I have an apartment back in Georgia, but the truth is, I spend my time at Max's place.

"Just recently, we made plans, and he knew I was coming into town, but an hour before I was set to arrive, he unexpectedly canceled. Fueled by curiosity and anger, I decided to show up anyway. Upon arriving, I spotted his car parked in the lot, and I could hear his cell ringing inside the apartment.

"I was so angry; I didn't deserve this to happen to me again. I didn't mean to kick his door down. I guess I didn't realize my own strength. 'No, correction, it was just a cheap ass door frame,' she said with a satisfying look that mingled with irritation.

"It felt like a moment right out of a movie. The door came crashing down, and I just bolted through it at full speed." Kimberley gasped and pressed her hand over her mouth in disbelief. "Summer, he picked me up and threw me out of his apartment like I was trash. A woman came rushing out of the bedroom, and he had the audacity to act like he needed to protect her from me! I have never been so humiliated. And here's the kicker, his chubby ass isn't even that good-looking."

A soft chuckle bubbled up inside Summer, trying not to burst out in laughter at Kimberley's expense. She was glad they were pulling into the driveway, hoping Kimberley would feel comfortable enough to share her feelings with Rose. Summer glanced over at Kimberley; she felt at a loss for words, unsure how to comfort her in this chaotic moment.

"Kimberley, I've pondered that question a million times. I don't know why we sometimes cross paths with evildoers before we find our prince. But sometimes, you just need to take a step back and allow love to genuinely find you. It might not feel like a blessing now, but you spared yourself a world of trouble down the road."

"Yeah, that's easy for you to say; you've got Mr. Prince Charming himself practically gift-wrapped beside you. Meanwhile, I'm over here collecting bad decision value meals with an extra-large helping of regret." Kimberley teased, a playful glint in her eye.

Summer couldn't help but smile, truthfully admiring Stevin for being one of a kind. "Your time will come, Kimberley," she reassured her. "But my advice is don't rush it, take it slow. Give yourself time to heal. Love can be messy and complicated. Take a page from your big sister's book; love can be dangerous."

Kimberley immediately piped up in her goofy way, "Now, sis, Christopher was a different story! We both know that man was fine and well-endowed. That dick was good enough to have any woman dicknotize, she said, bursting into laughter as she playfully slapped her leg.

However, her laughter quickly faded. Kimberley noticed Summer pulling away, a telltale sign she had crossed the line. "Too soon, huh? I'm sorry, I think I'll just exit now, she said, acknowledging that she hadn't read the situation correctly and her humor hadn't landed as she had hoped.

Summer slumped back into the driver's seat, exhaling deeply as she threw a sideways glance at Kimberley. Once the car door slammed shut, a soft giggle escaped her lips. She had to accept that Kimberley's inappropriate, quirky sense of humor was simply part of who she was, and no harm was meant.

CHAPTER: 18
I CHOOSE YOU!

Summer was overjoyed to learn that Stevin had decided to cut his trip short and return home. Just four days into his week-long trip, he found himself missing Summer and eager to reunite her with their son. His family's treatment of her only reinforced his realization that he chose her above all else.

Mr. Bash felt a heavy heart upon hearing about Stevin's abrupt decision to shorten his visit and return home earlier than planned. Stevin had clearly expressed to his father his disapproval of the family's treatment toward Summer, emphasizing that both Summer and his son were his top priorities. In a determined effort to heal the growing rift, Mr. Bash offered to drive Stevin and Asher back to Minnesota. He was resolute in his goal to mend his family, as he proposed turning Stevin's trip back home into a family road trip in his RV. However, his hopes were shattered when his wife refused to play nice. Mrs. Irene flatly refused to accompany him; she was unwilling to set aside her grievances and reconcile with Summer and her family.

Meanwhile, Camile was bubbling with excitement when she learned about the road trip. She was eager to spend time with Stevin and his son, and the chance to see Summer again filled her with a sense of anticipation for the family bonding that was about to take place.

***

Rose was delighted to host Stevin's family, with the exception of his snobbish mother. She was ecstatic to learn that Mrs. Irene would not be visiting. A wave of relief washed over her, as she had no desire to play nice or put on a facade.

On Thursday morning, the atmosphere in the house buzzed with excitement as Rose and Summer dedicated their day to transforming the home into a warm and inviting space. They decorated the living area with vibrant fresh flowers and prepared the kitchen for large family meals. Summer had shared with Rose about her visit to the farm, and there was no way Stevin's mom would outdo her in the kitchen.

Kimberley, eager to be the generous sister, willingly surrendered her own bed so that Mr. Bash wouldn't have to stay in a cramped hotel room. To make room for Camile, they also purchased a stylish queen-sized bed for Asher's nursery, ensuring that everyone would feel comfortable.

When David learned that Stevin would be returning with his family, he decided to postpone his trip home, with the understanding that Rose would travel back with him. They all agreed not to invite Papa Joe over for the sake of Rose and Summer. Additionally, when traveling, a family member would drive to an airport a couple of states over to ensure Summer's location remained safe.

***

The family gathered on the sun-drenched porch as they eagerly awaited the arrival of Stevin and his family. Summer's hands itched with anticipation, a mix of joy and longing; she couldn't wait to cradle Asher in her arms, vowing never to be separated from her son again. As the massive RV rolled up the driveway with her family in it, she couldn't contain her emotions as she missed Stevin just as much.

When Stevin finally stepped off the RV, cradling their son like a football, he carried him like a prized possession, his grin wide enough to light up the evening. Summer rushed down the steps, her heart racing as she prepared to embrace them, extending her arms and reaching for Asher.

With a mischievous glint in his eyes, Stevin teasingly blocked her access to him, a comically exaggerated expression of offense on his face. "Now, woman, surely you're not going to greet me like this?" he said, turning his body to block her from Asher. "Little lady, the only way to this kid is a big wet kiss on my lips," he declared, puckering his lips comically as if he were presenting an award.

Summer leaped onto her tippy toes, stretching to reach his lips, giving in to his playful antics. As their lips met softly, he felt a rush of warmth. He relaxed, and his hold on Asher loosened. She eased him out of Stevin's arms, and the moment she had a good grip, she turned away, cuddling and kissing him, leaving Stevin standing speechless. He turned towards his dad with a theatrical gesture, throwing his hands up.

Laughter erupted around them as the families exchanged warm greetings while Stevin busily unpacked the RV. Summer could hear the commotion of everyone getting acquainted as she sat nearby, her heart full as she gazed at her son, tracing every detail of his face, observing him inch by inch, feeling as if he had grown over the week.

Mr. Bash and Camile, standing off to the side, watching the scene unfold with knowing smiles, they didn't take it personally that Summer failed to greet them, understanding her preoccupation was simply a reflection of her love and concern for her son, having spent the entire road trip on FaceTime navigating the ups and downs of Stevin traveling with their infant son.

David felt a sense of familiarity and a return to normalcy; it had been over a year since he had fired up the grill, popped the top on a cold beer, and enjoyed some male bonding time. Despite the lavish feast Rose and Summer had prepared that would make any gathering memorable, nothing could deter David from seizing the opportunity to show off his grilling skills. Stevin and his father gladly relinquished the grilling duties to David, both preparing to stay out of the kitchen, whether indoors or outdoors.

Meanwhile, Kimberley and Camile wasted no time in forming a warm bond. A spark of connection ignited between them as they shared stories and laughter, Kimberley having already gotten acquainted with Josh's twin brother. The two exchanged glances while Camile was FaceTiming her husband. Their goofy behavior and budding friendship added a much-needed comforting touch to the family gathering.

The evening was alive with a much-needed vibrant energy that both families needed. Everyone was in good spirits as the ladies played Tug of War with baby Asher, each of them vying for the chance to keep him close throughout the night. Camile, visiting from out of town, felt she should have the first dibs on him by watching him overnight, yet Rose clung to her determination that her grandson would be nesting next to her.

In a quieter corner of the room, Stevin had made it clear to Summer that they needed some alone time, urging her to let the rest of the family take charge of the baby for the evening. Although Summer would have preferred to keep a watchful eye on her son, she knew she needed to devote some attention to Stevin and their relationship. Besides, she had a house full of family, and her son needed all the love the family was providing.

With the atmosphere thick with laughter and the clinking of bottles, Stevin, with a carefree demeanor, seemed to be consuming bottles of beer faster than the other men. Summer and the family had closely watched with a mixture of concern as he downed several bottles in a short time. To ensure Stevin didn't feel overwhelmed or judged, Camile and Kimberley were discreetly tasked with clearing the cooler of beers. David had purchased a 12-pack of beer with Stevin's father in mind, unintentionally overlooking Stevin's ongoing struggles with his own challenges.

Meanwhile, Stevin had other thoughts swirling in his mind. He craved a smooth, mellow buzz to set the perfect mood for the night, fueled by a growing determination to have Summer surrender to all his sexual demands. The night was just beginning, and he was intent on making it one to remember.

As the night deepened and a blanket of stars illuminated the sky, everyone began to retreat to their cozy sleeping arrangements one by one. Mr. Bash, ever the gentleman, couldn't bear the thought of displacing Kimberley from her warm bed. Instead, he opted for the solitude of the RV, a peaceful haven amidst the wilderness.

He relished the idea of roughing it in nature, feeling thrilled at the prospect of sleeping under the vast, open sky without his wife urging him indoors. The RV provided a peaceful retreat, removed from the bustle of the day-to-day drama and filled with the soothing, calming sounds of the night, the gentle whisper of the breeze and the distant calls of nocturnal wildlife. This setting made him long for more bonding time with his son, as he planned to suggest a campfire, and an outdoor camping experience under the stars for the following evening.

As he settled into the RV, surrounded by the fragrant scent of pine and the cool caress of the night air, Mr. Bash experienced a profound sense of peace washed over him. It was the perfect escape, a chance to immerse himself in the great outdoors and enjoy his desperately much-needed alone time.

CHAPTER 19:
MAKE LOVE TO ME

Summer reached out, her fingers gliding over the polished porcelain of the shower knobs as she turned them off, allowing the last droplets of warm water to trickle down her bare skin. She felt completely relaxed after absorbing the soothing heat of the warm shower, a perfect way to wind down after a beautiful day spent with her family.

Wrapping herself in a soft towel that clung to her damp body, she stepped out of the bathroom to catch a breeze, allowing the steam to dissipate, mingling with the calming scent of lavender body wash that filled the bedroom.

Standing by the bedside, she began to apply oil to her skin when she heard the bedroom door softly open and close. Summer could sense the unmistakable energy of Stevin's presence before she even turned around. Feeling an instant shift in the atmosphere that clung to her like a second skin. The air became thick with an electrifying tension of anticipation, wrapping around her like a warm, pleasurable tingle.

Notably, while she was showering, Stevin had stripped the room of Asher's much-needed essential items that he required throughout the night. He moved Asher's bassinet into the nursery, intentionally ignoring Rose's request, as he chose to honor his cousin's wish to spend some time with his son.

Stevin stood still behind her, his warm, minty breath tickling the sensitive skin of her neck, sending shivers down her spine. In a tender yet tense embrace, he wrapped his arms around her, the gentle rhythm of their bodies swaying in slow motion, creating a moment of connection amidst the chaos of their daily lives.

With a tender grip around her neck, he tightened his hold slightly. His fingers offering a comforting pressure as her head tilted back against the strength of his muscular chest. The warmth of his body enveloped her, creating an intimate cocoon. Summer opened her mouth to speak, her thoughts evident in the way her brow furrowed. Anticipating her concerns, Stevin leaned closer, his breath soft against her ear as he whispered, "Asher is fine." The warmth of his words seemed to comfort her raging thoughts, but he could feel another question bubbling up.

Before she could utter it, he swiftly covered her mouth with his hand, his finger tracing the delicate curve of her lips, silencing her unspoken worries. She slightly opened her mouth as his fingers traced the bottom of her lip and gently bit down on it before taking it into her mouth. She could feel his knees buckling as her warm wet mouth enveloped his finger, her tongue creating a sucking sensation and sending tingles throughout his body.

"Are you good?" he asked, ensuring he hadn't crossed any lines that could trigger her PTSD.

Summer nodded yes, feeling a magnetic pull as he drew her closer. He took a few steps back, their bodies instinctively moving in sync, as he guided her towards the bathroom.

She stood still in the softly lit bathroom like a shy schoolgirl, as Stevin released her from his grasp. He reached around her, his movement purposeful, and turned on the shower. The soothing sound of the water cascading down created a tranquil melody.

Wrapped in the comforting warmth of a towel, she felt the plush fabric brush against her ankles as it slipped away when Stevin tugged it loose, leaving her exposed to the anticipation of what was to come next. The air felt cool against her skin, heightening her senses. He gently lifted her chin, his fingers brushing against her jawline as he searched her eyes for any hint of hesitation. "Are you okay?" he asked again, his voice steady and reassuring. His gaze tense, locking onto hers with an unwavering focus as he slowly stood and began to undress, never breaking eye contact, deepening the connection between them.

Stepping around her, Stevin stepped into the shower first assisting Summer in behind him as he directed her to face him. Time stood still as they stood as the water poured down like a silken curtain, the steam swirling around them like a misty veil. Their eyes locked, and with a tender pull, he drew her close, their lips meeting in a soft, passionate kiss; the vivid, horrid images of Christopher began to fade away into distant memories.

She had always been attuned to his moods, able to sense when he yearned for a bit of indulgence. They stood motionless without him taking the lead, and neither one was willing to break the silence. She felt an irresistible pull toward him. With a gentle smile, she reached up, letting her fingers glide through the lush, springy curls of his soft hair, relishing the sensation as each strand slipped between her fingers. Stevin shifted his head slightly, his eyes ablaze with intensity. A playful smile danced at the corner of her mouth as she recognized the quiet exchange that spoke volumes without the need for words. She knew she was given the wrong body part the attention.

Stevin rested his hand on her head as he motioned for her to lower herself down. Summer eased to her knees, tracing her mouth against his wet skin. She paused for a brief moment, looking up at him before engulfing his entire swollen, throbbing manhood into her mouth. He stared intently at her, his mouth slightly open, as she enjoyed every moan that escaped him. He tilted his head back, resting it against the shower tiles as he enjoyed the tightening of her mouth sucking and squeezing up and down his shaft.

As she lifted her gaze to meet his, her eyes swept across his face; his expression lit up with undeniable pleasure. The fact that he was loving it gave her a rush of climatic chills that danced throughout her body. The deep longing to please him ignited like an unquenchable flame within her soul, consuming her every thought and driving her every action. Stevin could feel her desire to please him as both of his legs felt like spaghetti.

In an attempt to gain some control and assert dominance, he lifted her to her feet. The gentle approach that had guided his movement was long gone, slamming her back against the slick, cold shower tiles, the chill biting into her skin as the sound echoed in the confined space—ramming every inch of himself inside her at one time. A slight scream escaped her, but he couldn't stop himself; the tightness of her inner muscles gripping and massaging his pulsating dick took precedence at that moment. Summer's moans got louder, attempting to quiet her; he placed a face towel in her mouth for her to bite down on, his strokes getting deeper and more intense. She couldn't control the pleasuring screams that escaped her. Knowing they had a houseful, Summer begged him to stop and give her a moment.

Stevin eased her to her feet, his touch warm and steady against her cool, damp skin. In a seamless motion, he lifted her out of the shower; the steam clung to the air around them like a misty haze of lust. He wrapped her in a soft, fluffy robe and slipped into his navy pajama pants and tennis shoes. Snatching the car keys from the dresser, he swept her into his arms, her head resting against his shoulder as he carried her towards the car.

Stevin drove two miles down a winding road to a secluded wooded area, the silvery glow of the full moon illuminating his path. He brought the car to a halt, shifted it into park, and stepped out. With a sense of urgency, he opened the passenger door. Summer sat panting as the rush of anticipation overwhelmed her racing thoughts.

"Are you okay?" he asked, a mix of concern and excitement flickering in his eyes as he searched her face for signs of distress.

With a nod, she offered a reassuring smile, though her breath was still quick. Stevin stepped forward and effortlessly lifted her from the seat, placing her onto the warm, metallic hood of the car. The short drive provided some much-needed warmth to the cool metal. He removed her robe, exposing her nudity to the crisp breeze that surrounded her, causing her nipples to become erect. The whispering breeze danced around them, heightening the electric tension in the air. Stevin stood close, his fingers gliding over her body with a delicate touch, sculpting her curves.

Her yearning for him was so intense that it drained her strength, leaving her vulnerable to his sexual demands. With every purposeful stroke of his hand, she let out a moan, allowing a fleeting thought of Christopher to escape her and dissipate into the cool night air like mist at dawn. Her self-thoughts began to fade as if a painter had softly brushed over the vivid disarray of colors of her past. The pleasure she was receiving triggered a wave of memories of her happy life with Stevin. The final pieces of her complex life were replaced like a missing puzzle that had prolonged the completion of her next steps in her life. In their heated moment, she felt a sense of clarity wash over her, like a gentle tide revealing a hidden shore of rhythmic climatic waves as her muscles contracted and a wave of pleasurable sensation weakened her.

Stevin's heart ached for Summer to desire him with a passion that was unmatched. He needed nothing more than to feel the weight of her irresistible attention, free from the shadow of Christopher. As he drew closer, he brushed his lips softly against hers, sending a jolt of electricity through her.

His gaze locked onto hers, a piercing intensity that seemed to demand an answer. "Is there something you want to tell me? Do you desire me, Summer?"

A blush spread across her cheeks as she met his gaze, her heart racing. "With every fiber of my being, Stevin," she whispered, her voice trembling with sincerity.

"Can I have you as I desire you?" he asked, his eyes reflecting the depth of his longing as if he wished to reach into her soul and pull her closer.

"Do to me as you please."

"So, do you want to tell me something?" he pressed again.

Summer looked confused for a moment before realizing what he desired. She propped herself up on her arms, leaned in close to his face, and whispered in his ear, "She's yours, baby."

"And What?" he asked.

"Do to her as you please!"

"And What?" he asked again.

"Make love to me, Daddy."

"Rephrase your statement," he demanded.

"FUCK ME DADDY!"

Stevin tilted his head back, stretching his neck as a contented smile spread across his face. He savored her sweet words like fine wine. She was his fiancée, and tonight, he would ensure that the name Diamond faded into nothingness!

Stevin lifted Summer's leg, placing it on his shoulder. He kissed her feet, tracing his bottom lip from her ankle to her inner thigh, delivering small pecks that sent chills throughout her body. She craved so badly to feel him deep inside her. But he continued to tease her with sensual kisses all over her body.

Taking his tongue and circling her erect nipples, he placed his hand on her stomach, feeling the vibrations of her body; he could feel her labored breathing as she craved to release her built-up climax. Spreading her lips apart, he stiffened his tongue as he savored the taste of her juices. In a steady sucking motion, he sucked her clitoris between his lips as his grip on her clit became tighter. He sucked with such an intense brushing over her clit until her body exploded with orgasms. A wave of pleasurable screams echoed through the night air. She felt every inch of him desiring to make love to her until she begged him to stop.

Pulling her into him, gripping the back of her thighs, he controlled her movement as he thrust deep inside her, slamming his body into hers with each hard thrust. The louder the moans that escaped her, the deeper he thrust in and out of her. He slightly bit her lip to muffle her moans, but the vibration of her trembling lip and sexy sigh enticed him to go deeper.

Stevin started making low groans as his strokes became deeper and harder. He slid her down, flipping her onto her stomach as he dove deep into her inner muscle before letting out a roar into the night sky as he reclaimed what belonged to him!

CHAPTER 20:
ACCIDENT OR MURDER!

The days flowed by in a delightful rhythm, filled with laughter and the warmth of shared childhood stories as the families enjoyed one another's company. For the first time in what felt like ages, both families could take a deep breath, for a moment, let go of their worries, and immerse themselves in this beautiful moment. Whether cooking meals together, playing games on the lawn, or exchanging stories by the crackling fire, they could do so without the constant dread of looking over their shoulder.

Stevin felt as if he were floating on cloud nine. He enjoyed the normalcy and bliss of being with family, listening to baby Asher's soft coos and their shared laughter. The mouthwatering smell of a home-cooked meal filled the air, creating a cozy family atmosphere that wrapped around him like a warm blanket. Yet, amid this lovely gathering, a significant void weighed heavily on his heart: his mother. Despite the joy surrounding him, her absence felt like a missing piece of an intricate puzzle. She remained emotionally distant, unwilling to let go of her anger and join in the time spent with his extended family and her grandson.

On the other hand, a match made in heaven was forming. Kimberley and Camile were inseparable, like two peas in a pod, always together, whether tagging along with the man at the bar or hopping from one bar to another in the next town over. Rose and Stevin observed from a distance, concerned for Summer's emotional well-being.

When Kimberley first learned about Summer and discovered she had a big sister, she did everything except embrace her, rejecting all of Summer's attempts to connect while instantly bonding with Camile.

Knowing the situation likely caused Summer to feel hurt as she watched her sister bond so effortlessly with Camile when she had rejected her so coldly. Summer couldn't help but feel a sense of loss; their chemistry reminded her of her and Ebony's friendship, which she mourned deeply.

In typical Summer fashion, she smiled and tucked away her feelings while focusing on Asher. Besides, everyone was happy enjoying each other, and that's all that mattered. What more could she ask for in a moment like this, even if it meant masking her own emotions?

As the final day of the visit quickly approached, Summer graciously allowed Stevin to bask in his dad's presence, demanding little of his attention. Despite Stephanie's weekly reassurances that everything remained copacetic, Summer didn't miss a day searching the internet for her name and any familiar names she could remember linked to the Diamonds during her time of captivity.

Everyone's laughter and cheerful activities came to an abrupt halt, silencing the laughter that had filled the room when Summer released a piercing, panicked screech. The moment's joy shattered like glass as Stevin hurried to her side, concern etched on his face. Meanwhile, Rose stepped in, gently taking Asher from Summer's trembling arms as tears streamed down her cheeks, her sobs echoing the distress that gripped her heart.

Pointing frantically at the laptop screen, Summer's voice rose to a terrified scream, "He killed them! He Killed them!"

Stevin, taken aback by the moment's turn, leaned in closer, his brow furrowed with concern. "Who, Summer? Who?"

Kimberley rushed over, her hands swiftly snatching up the laptop. She set it back on the table, her breath hitching as her eyes widened with disbelief. "It's the bodyguard, Brody! He was the one keeping watch the morning she escaped." Her eyes reflected a mix of shock and fear, the weight of the revelation of Summer's worries and reality heavy in the air, paralyzing her for a moment.

Stevin walked away in a panic, frantically dialing Stephanie's number, with evident anxiety visible on his face. It wasn't long before he returned to Summer's side after ending the call.

"Summer, take a deep breath and calm down; Stephanie just confirmed it was a freak car accident, exactly as the news article reported," he urged, his voice steadier than his racing thoughts.

"No, Stevin, you don't understand! They helped me, Brody and his wife. He outright defied a direct order from Mr. Bash without hesitation, refusing to make me get dressed and visit Christopher, and a week later I go missing on his watch. No...no, Stevin," she said, her voice trembling as she nervously shook her head. "This isn't an accident." Summer insisted, her eyes wide with fear and conviction. "This was Christopher and his father."

Summer glanced up and saw the horrified look on Camile's face while Mr. Bash stood beside her, rubbing her arm. It was clear from Camile's expression that she realized the danger she was putting her beloved cousin in. All she wanted was to escape their stares.

"Maybe you're right, Stevin. I just need to take a nap. Mom, can you keep an eye out for Asher? I just need a moment."

Stevin, acting as her knight in shining armor, quickly scooped her up in his arms and carried her into the bedroom. She buried her face in his neck, finding comfort in his scent and the strength of his embrace.

He laid her down on the bed, but as he turned to walk away, Summer sat up and grabbed him by the hand. "I don't believe it was an accident, Stevin."

"Summer, just get some rest. Let's revisit this after your nap; give me some time to look into the matter."

Though Summer was far from sleepy, she just needed to remove herself from everyone's gaze, feeling like she was being stared at like a nutcase. She knew the Diamonds all too well, and deep down, she knew no matter what anyone said, this wasn't an accident.

Stevin returned to the family room, a wide grin spreading across his face as he tried to shake off the lingering tension and brush the incident away. The last person he needed to be added to the 'I Hate Summer Train' was his favorite cousin.

"Come on, little/big cousin! Let's seize the moment and create some lasting memories before you all hit the road."

Camile stepped forward, her expression empathetic as she informed him that Kimberley had shared the details of Summer's tumultuous past with Christopher, even her, involvement, and her heart broke for Summer. She softly reassured him that she would always be there to support them, no matter what they needed.

Meanwhile, Summer had fallen asleep, and everyone had chosen to let her rest, allowing her to sleep through the day. Five hours had passed, robbing her of precious time with Stevin's family.

She exited the bedroom and was surprised to find Kimberley snuggled up on the sofa, asleep with her head resting on Rose's lap. The soft hum of voices drifted in from the porch, pulling her attention. Curious, she eased to the door and peeked outside to find the entire Bash family sprawled comfortably in the rocking chairs, with Asher curled up on his grandfather's chest blissfully asleep. A serene smile stretched across Mr. Bash's face as he lightly taps Asher's back, soaking in the bonding time with his only grandson.

Stevin's boisterous voice rose above the chatter as he boasted about him and Orlando's latest lucrative investment, earning them a staggering quarter of a million dollars each. He animatedly discussed with his father the prospect of acquiring his dream car, a Bugatti. His former boss was selling his Bugatti for a steal, and he was determined to buy it. As she stood there eavesdropping, she learned that the entire family would be leaving out together. David and Rose would be dropped off at the airport, while Kimberley would continue traveling with Camile back to her home, where she had a date waiting with Josh's brother.

Summer quickly returned to the bedroom, digging into the closet and pulling out the black duffle bag containing the money meant for Mr. Jeffery. She hurriedly dashed upstairs to where she located David, packing for him and Rose.

"David, I don't ask for much, but I really need you not to fight me on this." Dropping the bag on the bed, she unzipped it, flashing the money inside. David's eyes widen.

"I need for you to take this cash and hire the best security company for you and Mom back in Atlanta, and also have a top-of-the-line security system along with fencing added around your parent's home.

"Before you say no, I just overheard Stevin downstairs bragging to his dad about a lucrative investment he made. Since half of what's being invested is my money, this is how I'm choosing to spend it. Get with Papa Joe and arrange for him to purchase a monthly cashier's check of $9500 throughout a five-month span. It's crucial that the amount remains under the radar to avoid any reporting issues or flags. Have him mail the check to your office addressed to you, using your clinic address. Take the rest of the cash, and instead of flying, I suggest you rent a car." Summer laid out a detailed plan to ensure her mom and David would be safe without David uttering one word. He simply agreed to her demands.

As everyone loaded onto the RV, Summer hugged each of them tightly. Rose cried and clung to her as David tried to soothe her fears. Rose knew she needed to return; David had already initiated the process of selling her home where she had spent the last three decades. He made it clear that it was unsafe and that his parents' home and location would be a safer option for them.

Camile was the last to hug Summer, her eyes glistening with tears as she softly whispered, "I know." With a warm smile, she added, "Whenever you and Stevin want to visit, my door is always open." She paused for a moment, then continued. "Just know my cousin has asked me to scout for some land near his parents' home. I thought you'd like to know about that." With a playful wink, she stepped back and walked away, leaving Summer guessing what Stevin had up his sleeve.

Summer and Stevin stood side-by-side on the porch, waving goodbye as the RV pulled out of the driveway. They exchanged a glance, their first moment alone since this ordeal began.

"Go get dressed, Summer." Stevin instructed casually, his tone light but firm.

Curiosity sparked in her eyes. "Why, Stevin? Where are we going?" she asked, tilting her head slightly.

He gave a playful grin, "Well, you don't have to get out, but you and Asher will be coming along for the ride. I need to make a quick trip to the store."

Summer furrowed her brow, perplexed. "What do you need from the store? We just stocked up on groceries before you got back."

Stevin chuckled lightly with a devilish grin. "It's not really about what I need; it's about what you will require after I'm through with you. By the time I'm done with you, you will be needing two to three Epsom salt soaks daily to soothe those muscles. Oh, and by the way, just so we're clear, there will be no tap outs. I'm about to bend you like a pretzel, he added"

With that, he turned to head inside, playfully smacking her on her backside as he walked past her. "Now, get to it, woman!"

CHAPTER: 21
OOPS' IT HAPPENED AGAIN!

Stevin fulfilled his promise by fully embracing every night they spent alone together. Summer relished in the magic of those moments, especially now with their new addition, Asher. It reminded her of simpler times when their world revolved solely around each other, blissfully tuning out the chaos of the outside world. The tranquil stillness around the house was lovely, and the freedom to roam around half dress or undress was much to Stevin's delight. Each evening turned into an intimate escape, where their passionate connection between them pulsated throughout the air, making every moment feel like a cherished bond that drew them closer.

Summer dove back into the rhythm of everyday life. Being under Rose's comforting presence, what had initially felt like a lifeline, now revealed itself to be a crutch to avoid pushing herself to cope with her new reality and start making the best of the situation, which she had done several times before.

Even Stevin appeared to have wrestled his inner demons into submission. He still enjoyed the comforting warmth of his favorite stiff alcoholic beverage of choice, but only in moderation that didn't warrant concern.

Three weeks had drifted by, and Rose was supposed to return to Minnesota two weeks ago. During each phone conversation with Summer, it seemed to paint a brighter picture as Rose listened to the joy and renewed hope blossoming in Summer's voice. It was undeniably clear that the time spent with Stevin and Asher had granted her the much-needed alone time to put herself together. David encouraged Rose to allow them the time alone they needed.

With a heart full of resolve, Rose agreed. She knew her family was safe and needed to start working on putting her life back together. Besides, she and David seemed to have reignited the spark, rekindling their love life, as she added a bittersweet end to a chapter of her life. Rose prepared herself to start over, making David's parent's house her new home, attempting to block out the feeling that she was living on a military base.

David's friends, fiercely loyal and protective, made it their mission to protect his family. Half the guys were retired from military service, so their connections proved invaluable. The money that Summer provided stretched further than David could have imagined, allowing them to turn their cul-de-sac into a secure residential area, providing a private security entrance. Everyone walked around with their service pistol; even David, who had never handled a gun, opted in to get one, and didn't leave home without it on his hip.

***

Summer sensed that Stevin didn't truly consider their current house a home. With her entire family living there, it felt more like a temporary living arrangement rather than a settled life. Determined to make the space feel more welcoming for him, she decided to undo some of the decoration decisions she and Rose had made. Instead, she utilized some of the photos and decor Stevin had brought back from the farm, which he had collected from their previous residence in Atlanta.

Feeling more at ease leaving the house, Summer and Stevin went shopping together, adding their personal touch throughout the home with previous family photos and photo's of Asher on the walls throughout the home. In her element, Summer even put her green thumb back to use by planting flower gardens around the yard, improving the landscaping, and making the house feel more inviting.

***

Rose sat in her cramped airline seat, she couldn't believe she had allowed herself to be away from Asher for sixty days; what had started as a one-week trip had turned into two months. The plane couldn't land fast enough.

Meanwhile, Stevin and Summer, like energizing bunnies, made sure to take advantage of every precious moment of solitude they had, before the rest of the family arrived in mere hours.

Kimberley, having arrived a few days earlier, opted to stay at her grandfather's house to spend some much-needed quality time with him. She was hiding the fact that she had brought her new boyfriend, Justin, along to meet him. Kimberley used the excuse that she would need a larger vehicle, Papa Joe's truck, to pick her parents up from the airport. So it would be more convenient to stay at his home. Hiding the fact, Justin's flight departed ten minutes before her parents landed at the same airport.

In typical Kimberley fashion, she couldn't contain herself; as soon as they arrived; before any proper greetings could be exchanged, she spotted Summer joyfully skipping toward the car, excited to see them.

"Well, dang, somebody's got a new walk! Looks a little gap legged to me," Kimberley remarked, her eyes playfully roving over Summer as she surveyed her from head to toe.

Rose shot her a warning look, hoping Kimberley would keep her inappropriate comments to herself. Stevin chose to bypass Kimberley, ignoring her teasing altogether and instead turned his attention to Rose, cradling sleepy Asher in his arms as he handed him off to her.

Kimberley pressed on, unfazed by Rose's piercing glares. "Dang, look at this yard, peeps! Stevin has really been putting it down, made this girl develop quite the green thumb," she said, swaying her hips back and forth.

"Dammit, Kimberley!" David shouted.

"What? We're all grown?" she shot back, a teasing smile spread across her face.

Stevin eased behind her, adding, "Not so grown that you snuck Justin down here and hid him from your parents."

Kimberley cut her eye's at him, "That damn cousin of yours talks too much!" a mischievous grin breaking through her annoyance.

Rose smiled as she entered the home; she enjoyed the fact Summer had made the home to her liking. When Kimberley entered before she could utter a word, as her mouth dropped when she saw the new decor Summer had chosen. David quickly warned her to keep her comments to herself.

The family went right back into their regular routine. Kimberley locked in her room, texting on her phone, and the men on babysitting duties watching the game while Summer and Rose cooked.

Summer took a couple of steps back from the stove as it looked as if she was about to faint. Rose let out a scream that alerted everyone. Asher was startled as he began to cry; Kimberley rushed down the stairs, attending to Asher as Stevin and David ran to Summer's side.

"I'm okay," Summer repeated as Stevin scooped her up and placed her in a chair at the dining room table. "I just got overheated. Can I please have a glass of cold water?"

The incident shook everyone up. Stevin remained at the table next to Summer while Kimberley assisted Rose with preparing the dinner plates. Before Rose could get the plate in front of her, the scent of the gumbo hit Summer's nostrils. She immediately covered her mouth, ran to the bathroom, and vomited. Everyone looked at each other as Stevin handed Asher off to Kimberley to attend to Summer.

David grabbed him by the arm, "No, son, we need to make a quick trip to the pharmacy. Let Rose and Kimberley assist Summer."

"What are we picking up, some medication for nausea?" Stevin asks with a clueless look on his face.

"No, son," David said, a knowing smile creeping across his lips as he shook his head. "More like a pregnancy test."

Stevin stood there, motionless, looking dumbfounded.

"I tried to tell y'all they been knocking boots since we been gone," but nobody wanted to listen to me, Kimberley mocked.

"Oh, child, hush and go take your sister some towels," Rose said.

Stevin remained in a daze as he kept repeating, "How?"

David glanced over at him, with disbelief on his face that Stevin was surprised at the fact this could happen.

"Son, have you guys been practicing safe sex?"

"Well, no! We went years without using protection, and she never got pregnant."

"Well, son, you woke up that sleepy monster when she got pregnant with Asher. You play grown-up games, and you get grown-up prizes.

Meanwhile, Summer sat in stunned silence when the man returned. With trembling hands, she took two pregnancy tests. Both sticks displayed the same undeniable answer: she was pregnant. Like Stevin, the reality of the situation left her dizzy; she couldn't understand how it happened so fast, giving her family a true welcome home surprise.

CHAPTER: 22
PLAYING WITH FIRE

In the initial weeks after learning about the pregnancy, Summer and Stevin found themselves immersed in a thick haze of uncertainty, a cloud of mixed emotions left them feeling disoriented. Their minds swirled with doubts, and their world felt surreal until the moment they stepped into the small, welcoming clinic for her first prenatal visit. The walls were adorned with parenting-themed artwork, and the soothing scent of lavender filled the air, offering a sense of calm. Her OBGYN, a trusted family friend who understood their situation, helped them feel at ease during the visit, allowing them to enjoy their time in the clinic without feeling anxious.

With Stevin's reassuring presence beside her, Summer inhaled deeply, her heart racing with anticipation as they settled into the examination room. The soft hum of the ultrasound machine created a backdrop to their nervous excitement. When the doctor turned on the ultrasound machine, the screen flickered to life, revealing their baby's tiny, pulsating heartbeat. In that instant, a wave of joy surged through them; they both grinned, fully embracing the thrilling reality of their new bundle of joy.

This pregnancy felt different; every moment of discovery became a cherished memory they shared together. Stevin lovingly measured her growing belly each week, marveling at the transformation of her figure as her baby bump blossomed. At twenty weeks, Camile and Kimberley surprised her with a gender reveal party, where vibrant pink smoke billowed into the sky. At that moment, their sweet baby girl received her name: Zoey Nicole Bash! Although it was a joyous occasion, it was overshadowed by Mrs. Irene's absence, as she still refused to accept Summer and her situation.

Meanwhile, Kimberley had finally mustered the courage to introduce Justin to her parents, exposing a vulnerability she had long kept hidden. Rose and David began spending more time back in

Georgia, aligning their life and current situation with the move. Life seemed simple, and things appeared to be coming together for them.

Even in the quiet house, despite Summer's family's absence, Stevin was determined to move his family closer to home and repair the relationship between Summer and his mother. After much discussion, Summer agreed to allow him to travel back home with baby Asher to visit his parents again. Energized by this opportunity, Stevin set his plan in motion.

He had recently acquired a vacant parcel of land ideally situated less than ten minutes from his parents' home, strategically placing the deed in Orlando's name to maintain discretion. This decision was part of his larger vision for their future, where he could raise his kids surrounded by family.

He planned to meet with the developers to discuss the exciting prospect of breaking ground on their new home. However, secretly, weighing heavily on his mind was another plan: he intended to get Asher paternity tested. His aim was to send the test results to Mr. Diamond, with the hope that the truth would illuminate the situation, that Asher wasn't his grandchild. Stevin believed this revelation could finally end the ongoing conflict between them and restore peace to their lives.

Unbeknownst to Stevin, Summer was fully aware of his carefully crafted plans to uproot her and the babies to Washington. Camille believed that Stevin's plans would unfold much smoothly if Summer knew the truth. After all, a monumental decision was being made regarding her life without her consent. Camille also had her own hidden agenda in telling Summer; she would be getting her favorite cousin back home with his family, and having the babies closer to her was an added bonus.

Summer was actually thrilled about returning to the farm with the hopes that she could mend her relationship with Mrs. Irene. After all, if she could navigate the complexities of her relationship with Kimberley, surely she could invest the same determination and effort into repairing her connection with Stevin's mother.

Feeling secure in Mr. Bash's connections, Summer felt a deep sense of security that she would be able to shield herself and her children from the Diamonds. Stevin's investments provided an added layer of reassurance; they could fly under the radar and still be in a safe place of comfort, and the farm offered just that.

For years, all she had dreamed of was getting married on the farm, bathed in the warm glow of a breathtaking sunset that painted the sky, and the golden fields that stretched endlessly. She longed for the day when Stevin would experience those cherished moments with both of his parents, enjoying time with their grandkids, just as her parents had done with Asher.

***

Seven and a half months pregnant, Summer was glowing, her skin shimmering with the joy of impending motherhood. Meanwhile, Rose remained in Atlanta, bustling with preparations to travel to Minnesota, where she would spend the next three months assisting Summer with the babies. David, on the other hand, would remain behind, starting his own practice; he wasn't in a position to take time away from work. Kimberley had stayed at the home with Summer to prevent her from being alone, while Stevin was back home visiting his parents.

It was music to Kimberley's ears as she eavesdropped on Stevin and Summer's conversation. Stevin had a candid discussion with his parents, particularly Mrs. Irene. Mr. Bash took sole responsibility for keeping Summer's past a secret from her. He explained to her what had happened the night of the engagement and why Summer was so distant.

Mr. Bash informed her that Summer told him she couldn't move forward with her engagement to Stevin without his parents knowing the truth. That when she confided in him about her past, he had forbidden her from discussing it any further, requesting that she bury her past and her worries, and not to bring it up again. This revelation seemed to open the door for more conversation. Stevin also revealed to his mom that he had purchased some land not far from them, making it clear that if she wasn't willing to accept him and his family entirely, he wouldn't move back.

With that revelation, Mrs. Irene requested to speak with Summer over the phone. However, Stevin refused her request, suggesting that his mom speak with Summer in person instead. He saw this as the perfect opportunity to fly Summer out and inform her about his plans to build a home on the land he purchased. Before calling Summer and informing her of the plans for her to fly out and meet with his mom, he reached out to his best friend Orlando, asking if Summer could use his wife Addison's digital ID to scan at the airport.

Summer didn't put up much of a fight; she was still as nervous as before to use Addison ID despite the striking resemblance. Even more anxious that she wouldn't have Stevin by her side. Kimberley had vowed to keep the TSA officer distracted with her humor as she would be flying out with her. Due to Summer's size, the doctor was afraid of her delivering a large baby, and she had an important ultrasound scheduled to measure the baby's size to determine if she needed a second cesarean section.

CHAPTER: 23
WHY ARE YOU BEING SUCH A BITCH!

Summer settled into the creaking rocking chair on the porch, her hands gently caressing her round, growing belly. The day felt peaceful as a gentle breeze blew through her disheveled hair. With no one to impress and Stevin still away, she rarely bothered to change out of her Mumu. She glanced down at her belly, feeling a bit anxious about her upcoming appointment. She preferred to have a vaginal birth and prayed that her body wouldn't react like it did before, leaving her in a coma.

Suddenly, she looked up and saw Kimberley's car speeding up the driveway; her heart dropped. Clearly, something was wrong. Summer struggled to stand quickly to her feet.

Kimberley hopped out of the car with a bright smile; nothing about her demeanor screamed danger.

"What's wrong, Kimberley? Why are you driving so fast?"

Kimberley bounced onto the porch quickly, passing Summer up as she playfully jiggled her stomach.

"Come on, belly! We have to pack up and leave early. There's a massive winter storm headed our way that could potentially shut down the highways."

Summer wobbled into the house behind her as dread seeped in. "No, Kimberley! What about my appointment?"

"Summer, it's a blizzard; no doctor's office will be open. Just call Shannon directly; she will inform you of this. Right now, we need to focus on packing."

As rising anxiety swirled in her chest, Summer felt her heart pounding like a bass drum. Thoughts raced through her mind, and everything seemed to be moving too fast. She nervously dialed her cousin's personal cell with trembling fingers. Shannon answered, her voice laced with concern as she confirmed the storm's severity. She mentioned that the office would be closed on Thursday, but if she was particularly worried about traveling, she could attempt to squeeze her in tomorrow for her ultrasound, though she couldn't promise a time.

Summer's legs felt heavy as she struggled to climb the stairs, each step leaving her more breathless than the last. She located Kimberley in her bedroom, packing.

"Sis, Shannon will see me tomorrow. I'll be packed and ready, so we can head straight to the airport from the doctor's office."

"No, Summer! By then, we are taking a chance of being stranded at the airport if the planes are grounded. We need to leave tonight! I've already switched my flight. Here, take my phone; I'm still logged in so that you can change yours."

Anger surged through Summer; she flung Kimberley's phone onto the bed. "Why would you change your flight without even discussing it with me? This isn't just any trip. This is my life, my child's life that's at stake! I can't just jump up and move around like you without planning it out. This ultrasound is vital for me, why can't you grasp the gravity of that?"

"Summer, it's just a checkup! Josh and Camille said they could get you scheduled for a 3D ultrasound while you're there."

"And there it is, this is all about Justin, isn't it? Screw my life and the well-being of your niece! I was just waiting for your true colors to show, your selfish side to emerge!"

"Are you serious Summer, I have bent over backwards kissing your ass attempting to repair our relationship!" Kimberley shouted, tears streaming down her face.

"Hm. Oh really! Or was it just the mere fact that the entire family shunned you, and you had no choice?"

Kimberley's face flushed with anger as she clenched her fists and turned to Summer, shouting "Why are you being such a, BITCH"

Summer swiftly turned on her heels and exited the bedroom in a flurry of emotions. She could hear Kimberley screaming into the phone, while David and Rose's voices echoed through the speaker as she made her way down the stairs. Kimberley sounded distraught as she explained to her parents what had occurred. Summer could hear Rose comforting Kimberley, making excuses for her emotional state and attributing it to her PTSD, as if her own well-being and that of the baby's weren't also important factors.

Summer stormed into her room and slammed the door, locking it behind her. She felt her phone vibrating beneath her, but she didn't need to check to know who was calling. Pulling her phone from under herself, it buzzed again in her hand. Summer glanced at the screen and saw her mother's name glaring back at her. Rose had called three times, and now Kimberley was pounding on the door like a 10-year-old child who had snitched to their parents.

"Summer! Mom wants to talk to you!" Kimberley yelled through the door.

In a fit of stubbornness, Summer allowed Kimberley to knock several times before she gave up and walked away. Her phone buzzed again, and it was Stevin.

"Hello," she answered, her voice barely above a whisper.

"What's going on, baby? Why are you fighting with your sister and ignoring your mom's call?" Stevin's voice was soothing yet stern.

Tears streamed down her cheeks, telling Stevin the events that occurred. "I just won't be able to come, Stevin. I have to know that my baby and I are okay."

"Baby, take a deep breath and calm down. I can leave Asher with my parents, and I'll come home so we can fly out together," he said, trying to comfort her.

"No, Stevin! Let's just wait until after Zoey is born. I can't take this stress. And besides, there's some bad weather coming in, possibly a blizzard. That's why Kimberley left me."

"Summer, can you tolerate a day's drive?"

"No, Stevin! You can't drive in these conditions!"

"Summer, my dad was once stationed in Alaska. I'm pretty sure he's well-trained to handle hazardous driving situations."

"Stevin, please, let's just wait."

"Summer, I need you here; please, this is important to me."

Summer could hear the disappointment in his voice as he pleaded with her for cooperation. She was overwhelmed with conflicting emotions. On one side was Stevin, persistently asking her to join him, while on the other, Rose's relentless texts urging her to leave out with Kimberley. Overwhelmed, she finally gave in to Stevin's request to travel back with him and his dad, all while texting a response to Rose.

"No, Mom. I need to make sure my health and the well-being of my child are okay before I travel. Everyone seems to forget I was in a coma for a week after Asher's birth. Please don't worry, Stevin is on his way back."

Rose simply texted back, "Okay."

Frustrated, Summer hurled her phone across the room, burying her head in her pillow. She was later jerked awake by the sound of Kimberley's car tires screeching against the pavement as she sped out of the driveway. In a panic, she quickly leap out of bed, her heart racing, as she activated the alarm, hastily moving around the house, snatching all the curtains closed, while wedging heavy chairs against the doors to ensure her safety.

Later that evening, Summer was once again awakened from her sleep by relentless tapping on the doors and windows. The sound echoed throughout the large, empty, quiet home. As she groggily stood up, a wave of unease washed over her. She eased to her feet and slowly tiptoed to the front door, her heart pounding in rhythm with the frantic knocking. Pressing her ear against the cool wood door, she caught the muffled sound of a deep, rusty male voice.

"Rose darling, she's not answering; I don't want to frighten her," the voice rumbled, laced with concern.

Instantly, Summer recognized Rose's frantic voice, demanding her father to hammer harder on the door. A wave of anxiety gripped her: the fact that Rose had personally reached out to her father made Summer's stomach twist into knots at the thought of how worried she must have been.

Slowly opening the door, Summer was speechless. Her grandfather stood before her, his wrinkled hands, and gentle eyes that mirrored the warmth of Rose's, accompanied by a kind smile.

"Hun, she's okay; I have my eyes on her now," he assured, attempting to calm Rose.

Summer could hear Rose's distant shouts crackling through the phone as she demanded that her father put Summer on the line. Yet, Summer's feet felt heavy, as if they were cemented to the floor, lost in her grandfather's sorrowful gaze. Oddly, she didn't feel hatred towards him as he looked at her with such sorrow.

"Grandad didn't mean to scare you, hun; I have your mother on the phone," he said, gently handing Summer his cell.

With shaky hands, Summer brought the phone to her ear. Rose's voice erupted from the speaker with worry and urgency. "Why haven't you answered me?!" she shouted. Summer responded softly, "Maybe my phone is dead."

"Summer, you have to leave now with Dad; your appointment has been canceled. The storm is approaching faster than what was expected. You'll be snowed in!"

Despite this, Summer refused to leave, allowing Papa Joe to set up the fireplace and place extra wood in the home he had brought with him. They place multiple candles throughout the house. Meanwhile, Stevin was livid that Summer had refused to leave and denied her grandfather from staying over. He scrambled to book a flight, but the harsh reality was that all flights had been delayed or canceled, leaving Summer stranded in the growing storm.

Summer slowly opened her eyes to the bright glow of the sunlight creeping through the curtains, only to be startled by the sight of several missed calls lighting up her phone screen. A knot of anxiety twisted in her stomach; it seemed like everyone had been trying to reach her, including Kimberley.

The cool breeze wafting through the room left her feeling like a mummy wrapped up in blankets, trying to stay warm. The tip of her nose tingled like a frozen icicle, and she could sense the beginning of a runny nose. She dreaded pulling away the thick, warm blanket, exposing herself to the cold draft in the bedroom. However, baby Zoey's constant jabs, as if she were playing soccer with her bladder, made it clear she wouldn't be getting comfortable until she emptied her bladder quickly.

Just as she mustered the strength to wobble out of bed, peeling away the comfort of her warm blanket, her phone buzzed again, this time with Stevin's name flashing across the screen.

"Good morning, baby!" she answered, trying to inject some cheer into her voice despite her discomfort. "Give me a moment; your daughter has decided to use my bladder as a trampoline."

"Summer, please don't you dare hang up," Stevin's voice echoed through the speaker, layered with concern and a hint of frustration.

"I've been trying to reach you all morning. What's up with you not answering the phone lately?"

"I don't know, Stevin. Lately, I've been sleeping a little harder in the morning. It seems as if I can't find a comfortable sleeping position until after 3 a.m.," she said, her teeth chattering as she made her way out of the bathroom, reaching for her robe and seeking refuge from the cold breeze throughout the home.

"Summer, Pop, and I will be leaving soon to come pick you up. But given the hazardous road condition, I'm leaving Asher here with Mother to keep him safe."

"Absolutely not, Stevin! I'm staring out of the living room window right now. The snow has piled high, nearly covering the porch. Thankfully, I still have power, and the fireplace is still burning. I refuse to stress about you and your father's safety. It's just another added layer of stress I don't need. Besides, the skies are clear, and no new snow is falling. Let's give it a couple of days. If the situation changes, I promise I'll let that man drive me into town to a shelter with available medical care close by."

"What, man, Summer? Are you referring to your grandfather?"

"Yeah, him," she replied, frustration evident in her voice, still unable to give him a title that she felt he had long since lost the right to.

Stevin sighed, reluctantly agreeing to her request before they disconnected the call. He was determined to move heaven and earth to get to her; a snowstorm wasn't going to halt his efforts.

CHAPTER: 24
AND THE CRADLE WILL FALL

Summer restlessly tossed and turned, her body thrashing from side to side as she jolted awake from a dreaded nightmare that felt all too real. Her skin was slick with sweat. The dream was so horrid that, despite the cool air in the room, which was visible by breath vapors with every exhale, she was still drenched in sweat.

Her nightmares had returned, the haunting image of the cliff, the biting chill wind that nipped at her skin, and the bone-deep chill of the snow she clawed through in a frantic attempt to escape Christopher. Surely, her mind was playing tricks, amplifying her fears as she lay alone in the quiet house. The fact the eerie cliff was less than two miles down the road felt like déjà vu. It had been years since she first escaped Christopher, and yet this recurring nightmare was back. Why now?

Trying her best not to focus on her eerie surroundings, which mirrored her dream, she was overwhelmed by paranoia. Summer begged Stevin to beef up security around the farm and pleaded with him not to leave, especially with the baby. She refrained from sharing the reason behind her anxiety, keeping the details of the nightmares that plagued her.

Summer sat cozily by the window, her breath creating small clouds of vapor on the cold glass as she gazed out at a winter wonderland. Outside, large snowflakes danced and tumbled, settling onto the thick layers of snow on the ground. Through the swirling storm, she spotted her grandfather maneuvering through the deep snow to bring her some supplies. The storm was returning, and Rose and Stevin had ensured that Summer had everything she needed with the help of papa Joe.

The brief exchange between them was silent. She watched as the snowmobile vanished, leaving behind a frosty trail in the growing storm. A deep regret settled in the pit of her stomach, dreading not taking Kimberley's advice and leaving with her. Guilt gnawed at her; she was even more remorseful of how she had treated her, knowing an apology was needed.

Just then, her phone rang, slicing through the heavy stillness of the silent room.

"Hello, my dear," she answered, her heart leaping with joy at the sound of Stevin's voice. The cheerful babble of her sweet son's voice added an extra layer of warmth to her heart.

Summer eagerly requested Stevin to hang up and FaceTime her, as she could hear Asher responding to her voice through the speaker. Her heart raced at the thought of seeing his adorable, chubby, rosy cheeks. To her surprise, Stevin called her back, revealing that he was seated in his car, holding Asher in his lap in the front seat. It was very noticeable he wasn't on the farm.

Summer's anxiety began to swell, and she immediately began to panic as she couldn't help but scold Stevin for being so reckless.

"What are you thinking?" she questioned, questioning the whereabouts of the security personnel, who was very noticeably absent. The unsettling realization that Stevin was driving alone with Asher, away from the usual safety of their surroundings, made her heart race even faster. The gravity of the situation weighed heavily on her as she anxiously awaited his explanation.

"Summer, sweetheart, please take a deep breath and calm down. This is a small town, and my dad knows the entire police force. There haven't been any reported suspicious activities or vehicles lurking around."

"Stevin, I could care less about a report from a small-town sheriff's office when the Diamonds have the entire LAPD in their back pocket. You need to get our child back to the farm, Stevin. Why would your father and security allow you to leave without proper protection?"

"Look, Summer, to be honest, we can't afford that kind of constant security around the clock. I have some funds tied up at the moment, and with two kids to support, we need to be financially stable."

"What are you saying, Stevin? Please tell me you're not risking our son's life or your own just to prove a point to me!" Her heart raced, the very thought wrapping around her throat like a vise grip.

"Hell, no, Summer! That's why I'm calling you. I did something that I believe will help us out in this situation."

Summer watched as Stevin fumbled to unfold a piece of paper that Asher had a time with. As he attacked the paper, Stevin had to pry open his tiny, tight fist gently. Stevin revealed a document. She zoomed in on the writing of the letter; Summer could see it was an official paternity test confirming he was indeed the father of baby Asher.

"Summer, I had to rush to the clinic and pick up the results before Orlando left out for his flight. I am headed home to fax the paperwork over to him now, and he'll deliver it to Christopher's father's office while he's in California. Now he will know he and his family have no ties to you."

"Stevin, none of this matters until you're safely back at the farm with Asher. Now, please, Stevin!" Summer pleaded, the tightening in her chest growing heavier

"Okay, Summer. I'll call you back as soon as we're back home. I need to get him fasten into the car seat."

Stevin's voice began to fade as his voice became muffled. Summer felt a wave of despair wash over her as if she was sinking underwater, and the feeling of doom overwhelmed her. Gathering herself, she raised her voice, desperation spilling over.

"No, Stevin! Do not hang me up! Drive. Just drive, and I will remain on the phone."

"Hold on, Summer, I've got to buckle him in." Stevin placed the phone down on the seat as the screen went blank, the line crackled, and for a brief second, his voice became distant. When his voice became more clearer, Summer could hear Stevin say, "What the heck?"

"What's wrong, Stevin?" Panic surged through her.

"Hold on, Summer. Someone just pulled directly behind me, blocking me in." She could hear the unease creeping into his words.

"Just get back in the car, Stevin, and wait until they move," she urged, though her voice felt as if it were slipping away into the void.

In the next chilling moment, she heard Stevin ask, "Can I help you?" Followed by the soul-chilling sound of a single gunshot that shattered the tense air. Asher's terrified screams pierced the air; a raw sound of terror echoed before his tiny voice was abruptly cut short, fading into a haunting silence, replaced only by the shrill roar of a speeding car as it tore away. Summer's world collapsed around her; she felt herself crumple to the floor, her body colliding with the wall as if time had frozen. "Stevin! Stevin!" she screamed, the anguish in her voice reverberating through the empty space, but there was no response.

In a frantic blur, she added a call to the line dialing Mr. Bash, merging him onto the call, her voice choked with sobs. He urged her to calm down, his comforting tone battling against her torment as he struggled to comprehend her desperate cries.

CHAPTER: 25
GONE IN A SECOND

"Something has happened! Something has happened!" Summer cried out, her voice trembling with panic and fear. Mr. Bash felt his heart plummet into his stomach as an icy dread washed over him, every instinct screaming that the news about to unfold was far from good. Her frantic screams echoed in his mind, instantly transporting him back to the battlefield horrors he had witnessed. The violent devastation of entire villages, the anguished wails of victims' loved ones screaming out in desperation and void. Yet, he couldn't allow his mind to go there.

"Summer, I need you to take a deep breath and calm down. Talk to me, young lady! What exactly has happened? he urged, his voice crawling with fear.

"He's not responding! I heard a gunshot! I can't hear him or Asher's voice anymore. The call is still active; I'm still on the phone with Stevin!" she cried out while continuing to scream out for Stevin to answer.

As Mr. Bash listened intently, every muscle in his body tensed as he strained to catch every detail. Stevin's FaceTime call was still connected, and they both could hear the unmistakable sounds of chaos, distant screams, and blaring sirens of emergency vehicles cutting through the air. His heart raced as he realized the gravity of the situation.

Suddenly, his phone beeped, alerting him to an incoming call from his good friend, sheriff Taylor.

"Summer, hold on for just a moment. I have an important call coming in," he said, quickly placing her on a brief hold before answering the sheriff's call. He held the phone to his ear, silent and tense, bracing for the words that would shatter his world — only to be informed that his son had been involved in a serious accident and that his immediate presence was required. A wave of urgency swept over him, mixing with the dread that simmered in his stomach.

Mr. Bash returned to the call with Summer; he held the phone without uttering a word. Summer recognized that he had returned to the line as the sound of the truck's roaring engine blared through the phone as he raced to get to the scene.

As Mr. Bash sped towards the scene, the local police officers stationed at the barricades spotted his truck approaching. Understanding the urgency, they quickly moved the barriers, creating a clear pathway, allowing him to drive directly up to the scene. Amidst the chaos, sheriff Taylor emerged like a roaring storm rushing in his direction, urgency etched on his face. He sprinted toward the truck, his voice rising above the chaos around them.

"Stop him! Stop him at once!" he shouted to his officers. "What were you thinking, letting him rush into the crime scene?" he bellowed, his tone laced with authority and distress.

"I specifically request that you hold him at the barricades and notify me as soon as he arrives! My God, this is his son!" he yelled, frustration and concern evident in his voice.

Mr. Bash spotted Stevin's car, igniting a fire within him. With every ounce of his 265-pound 6'2" stature, he surged forward like a freight train, barreling through several officers who tried desperately to restrain him. Sheriff Taylor attempted to calm him.

"Dammit, Steve, look at me! I need you to calm down and focus on me so we can help you,"

"It's my son, 'T.' Goddammit, let me go! Is that my son in the back of that ambulance? Let me loose so I can be by his side!" he roared, desperation fueling his every word while still dragging the officers behind him as they clung onto him with all their might. Still, with a tight grip on his cell phone, Summer listened closely, praying to hear the words that Stevin and her son were okay.

Amid the chaos and shoving, Mr. Bash was wrestled to the ground, his phone pressing uncomfortably against his chin. With a swift turn of his head, he had a clear few underneath his son's car when he spotted Stevin's shoes peeking out from under the blue tarp that covered his body. In that surreal moment, time seemed to freeze, and a haunting ringing filled his ears, drowning out the turmoil around him.

Overwhelmed, he let out a gut-wrenching scream that cut through the noise. "Is that my son lying on the ground?" The words echoed, desperate and raw.

A heavy, suffocating silence followed, as no one would answer, and everyone began to back away when he started sobbing, asking everyone, "Why isn't anyone from EMS helping my son?"

Each word was a plea, a cry for answers in the face of an unbearable reality.

"Damn it, Taylor! Our boys were raised side by side; you practically helped my wife raise my boys, and this how you honor him?"

Mr. Bash sprang to his feet; his face flushed with anger as he stormed toward Stevin's still lifeless body, "This is my damn son! Now help him, dammit!" he screamed at the officials on site.

No one moved; sheriff Taylor stepped towards him, gently placing his hands on Mr. Bash's shoulders, stopping him with his steady presence. He leaned in, resting his forehead on his, creating a moment of calmness that seemed to slow him down.

"He's gone, Steve, he's gone," sheriff Taylor said as Mr. Bash's knees buckled. Sheriff Taylor stood sobbing as he attempted to comfort his long-time friend.

"No, Taylor! Hurry, send them over there now to help him!" Mr. Bash shouted, his voice cracking with disbelief as he pushed forward, desperately trying to reach his son. His heart raced with worry, and each passing second felt like an eternity as he scanned the chaotic scene around him, hoping for a glimpse of help on the way.

Taylor collapsed to his knees, "He's gone, my good friend, he's gone," he said as he began to sob uncontrollably. He was executed, one fatal shot," he added, his voice barely breaking through the deafening noise of sirens and panicked voices. He cradled his childhood friend in a heartbreaking embrace, both of them lost in the devastation of their shared loss.

Mr. Bash tightly clutched Taylor's arm with a force that emphasized his growing panic; his knuckles lightened with tension due to his firm grip. Deep lines marked across his forehead and around his eyes spoke volumes of his distress.

"My grandson! Where's my son's child?" His voice quivered, and his hands trembled violently as if the weight of his fears was almost too much to bear.

"Steve, he's missing."

"What do you mean he's gone?" Mr. Bash's voice rose, filled with disbelief and dread.

"Your grandson has been abducted," Taylor responded, his voice low as he struggled to maintain eye contact with Mr. Bash. "I spoke with the clinic staff, and they confirmed that Stevin did have his son with him when he arrived at the clinic. I've already alerted the FBI, and they've initiated an Amber Alert. I used the latest photos you sent me of him playing on the farm."

"Dammit, Taylor! You know who is behind this! I want him... I want that son of a bitch now!" Mr. Bash's eyes were ablaze with a mixture of emotions: anger, emptiness, and a fierce determination to revenge his son. He was ready to confront the darkness that threatened his family, and he had nothing to lose.

"I understand, my friend," Taylor replied, his voice layered with empathy and concern. I've already briefed the FBI on Stevin and Summer's case using the information you previously provided, and we'll do everything we can to find him."

"Oh my God, Taylor! Summer, his fiancée, is on the line. Where's my phone?" Panic gripped him as the weight of the situation crashed down on his heart like a ton of bricks. "She's pregnant and all alone. She's heard everything; I must get in touch with her parents. She will need all the support she can get"

"Steve, the FBI agent, needs to speak with her right away. I can't even begin to fathom what your family is going through, but time is not on our side. We need to move quickly to locate your grandson."

Mr. Bash sank back to his knees, the world around him blurring as tears streamed down his face. The stark reality settled heavily in his chest: he would have to break the heart-wrenching news to his wife that their son was dead.

Summer had indeed overheard everything, every fanatic cry and sorrowful murmur echoing through the tense atmosphere. When the officers tackled Mr. Bash to the ground, his phone slipped from his grasp, leaving her still on speaker. She could hear some of the local officers expressing their condolences for the Bash family. Their voices carried a mixture of disbelief and frustration as they addressed their commanding officer, who demanded to know why they had allowed a family member of the victim to be present at the crime scene, especially before learning that their loved one had passed away.

One officer, with his brow deeply furrowed and voice strained, muttered, "We didn't know, John. We thought the sheriff had already spoken with him, informing him that his son was deceased and that his grandson was missing."

CHAPTER: 26
A DREAM OR REALITY

"Calm down, baby girl; I'm here," Rose's father reassured her. "The storm has really picked up, so I will have to stay with her until the weather clears, and you guys can come be by her side."

"No, Joe! She needs to be brought closer to town. You must get her to leave with you, now!"

"Rose, my dear, that's simply not possible. The storm has intensified, and the snow is swirling in relentless gusts. I can barely see a foot in front of me, and besides, I'm on a one-seater snowmobile. I had no choice; this one is equipped with a GPS tracker for my safety. I've already notified the emergency team to keep an eye on my location."

He could sense the concern in her silence on the other end of the line, knowing that the only peace he could provide was ensuring her daughter's safety and comforting her in her time of need. Not wanting to frighten Summer, he started with a light tap, speaking through the door softly, "Summer, it's me, Papa Joe. I've come because Rose and David asked me to come. You don't have to face this alone."

As the minutes stretched, tension mounted. "Rose, I'm afraid she's not answering, " he finally said, worry lining his voice.

"Break the window, kick the door down! I don't care what you have to do; just make sure she is okay," Rose insisted.

"Wait, hold on a second," he cautioned, his eyes scanning the snow-covered ground. "Someone has been here." A sudden dread, thick and suffocating, gripped him as he noticed tracks in the snow, the shoeprints far too large to belong to Summer. A chill, colder than the snow around him, washed over him; Summer was not alone.

Concern laced his voice, sending a shiver down Rose's spine. "Dad, what's wrong? What do you mean?" she cried out, her heart racing.

Hearing her call him "Dad" ignited something deep within him that had lain dormant since she was a little girl. He could still picture her as a little girl, her wide eyes filled with adoration and wonder, gazing up at him as though he were her superhero. Pressing the phone against his chest, he inhaled deeply. For a moment, after decades of silence from her, she had finally recognized him as her father once more. That small word held the power for him to bridge the chasm of time that had separated them.

"Rose, I need to check something out. Let me call you right back," he said abruptly before hanging up. He couldn't become emotionally distracted at that moment; his focus and only concern were the urgent need to follow the ominous footprints that veered off to the shadowed side of the home.

"Don't hang up!" Rose cried out, her voice breaking with fear. He had disconnected just as the weight of her worries crashed down on her—her son-in-law had been violently murdered, her grandson was missing, and now it seemed Summer was in direct danger. Panic surged through her veins. She had to reach her daughter, no matter the cost.

Papa Joe cautiously maneuvered his way back to his snowmobile, carefully stepping backward through the crisp, untouched snow that crunched beneath his boots. His eyes darted around, scanning his surroundings. Reaching into his weathered bag, he pulled out his hunting knife, the blade glinting sharply in the pale winter light. He activated the distress signal on the snowmobile.

With deliberate caution, he inched toward the side of the house, his heart pounding like a war drum in his chest. Gripping the knife tightly, he was prepared to protect the safety of his family at any cost. As he crept towards the back of the house, he heard a faint tapping on metal.

He slowly peeped his head around the corner, and he was suddenly struck in the face by a heavy object. Darkness enveloped him like a thick black fog. He briefly regained consciousness, realizing he was being dragged away from the house before he completely passed out.

Stevin Is That You

"Summer, Summer, wake up! You must wake up now," Stevin's voice echoed softly in her ear, a hunting whisper in the oppressive darkness she was feeling.

"Stevin, Stevin, where are you? I can't see you," she murmured, her voice fragile and trembling. Her eyes shot open wide with panic.

A sharp jolt of pain surged through her head, throbbing like a relentless drumbeat, a cruel reminder of the blow she had received. Cruel spasms seized her lower back, causing her to wince in agony. She was covered in a horrifying mess of her own vomit. As reality rushed back to her, dread settled heavily in her chest as memories flooded in. Mr. Bash's anguished cries echoed in her mind, and the officers' grim voices discussing the scene rang like a death knell, repeating the words: Stevin had been executed, and her son was missing.

The unbearable reality swept over her in waves. In that moment of overwhelming grief, the world faded away, and she lost consciousness. Her body slammed against the wall in a painful thud before collapsing onto the floor. The stress overtook her as she helplessly lost her stomach content while she was temporarily blacked out.

She felt utterly defeated; she had no fight left in her; this was all her fault. She had created this dangerous world that her entire family had been introduced to, and now her two main reasons for living were gone.

As she drifted into a fragile sleep, she sensed she could take her final breath, an eerie sense of calm settling over her — her will to live had dissipated into nothingness.

But then a voice pierced through the fog of her despair, clear and commanding: "WAKE UP!" It was as if Stevin were right beside her, shouting in her ear, jolting her back to reality. Her eyes snapped open once more as she was suddenly hit by an overwhelming stench of a musty odor mixed with the smell of damp smoke. It smelled as if the fireplace had been put out by water.

Summer felt the cold seep into her bones, leaving her stiff and shivering; she was pretty sure the roof had collapsed in, causing snow to put out the fire. An icy numbness clutched at her heart, rendering her unable to cry; every emotion felt muted, as if life itself had lost its meaning. Nausea twisted in her gut, and the pain was unbearable, yet she remained eerily still, trapped in her own anguish; she couldn't move.

She was startled by a sudden sharp crack in the floorboard that echoed through the silence. The sound sent her heart plummeting into her gut like a stone. Summoning every ounce of strength, she struggled to stand to her feet, her muscles protesting as she mustered up the strength to hoist herself upright. Bowing in pain, she crawled awkwardly towards the basement door, gripping the handle to lift herself up. Bent over in pain, she clung to the wall as she crept toward the front of the house.

The house was dark, as if maybe she had lost power to the house, but a faint glimmer from the plugin in the wall reassured her that she still had power.

A wave of fear coursed through her veins, sending shivers down her spine, and her teeth began to chatter uncontrollably due to the bitterly cold weather and the fear that gripped her. She peeled off her soaked shirt, attempting to stop the chattering noise to silence the sound.

As she stumbled through the pitch-black space, attempting to reach her bedroom at the front of the house, an inky shadow emerged before her, darkening the already black room further. Panic surged in, and with a scream that echoed through the emptiness, Summer's heart leaped into her throat—she was drowning in her own terror!

CHAPTER: 27
SHE'S MISSING

Rose paced nervously across the floor. With trembling hands, she dialed her father's and Summer's cell phones repeatedly until both of their lines stopped ringing and eventually started going straight to voicemail. She felt like she was drowning in sorrow, with no lifeline in sight.

On the other end of the line, Kimberley was frantic and hysterically crying; she desperately needed to be with her family, but there was no clear plan or direction, as it seemed her family was falling apart. Surrounded by the Bash family, she felt shunted, as if an invisible barrier had been erected around her. It seemed as if everyone treated her differently as if she didn't have the right to mourn Stevin's tragic death.

Mrs. Irene was a whirlwind of anger as she became manic, cursing the very ground Summer walked on. Meanwhile, Camile, grappling with her own grief, reeling from the loss of her cousin and best friend. She felt so overwhelmed that she couldn't even begin to process what had happened, let alone concern herself with how the other family was treating Kimberley.

Justin and Josh, who had known Stevin since grade school, and were like brothers to him, were also caught in their own tumultuous sea of grief. Their families were very close, and they also needed time to cope by being with the family and grieving during this devastating time. Justin even urged Kimberley just to return to his home until he returned from the Bash's home, offering her a semblance of emotional safety amidst the chaos that surrounded both families. Rose also had informed her that her grandfather and Summer were possibly in danger and couldn't be reached. This revelation hung heavily in the air, suffocating her with worry as they remained unreachable.

As Rose's world spun around her, she felt the walls closing in, and no matter how hard she tried to hold it together, she found it hard to breathe. In a moment of desperation, she suddenly began to spin in a circle, throwing her head back and letting out a piercing, hollow scream that was filled with raw anguish.

David rushed to her side, instinctively wrapping her in his arms, holding her tightly as if he were anchoring her against the storm, allowing her to express her anguish. Without uttering a word, he began to rock her gently as they both wept together. At that moment, the cruel reality of life felt insurmountable, as a dark shadow loomed over his family.

The shrill ring of Rose's phone cut through the tense silence, jolting David from his deep thoughts. He answered quickly, his heart racing, when Kimberley name appeared on the screen.

"Dad, where's mom? I need to merge you guys on a call; the Minnesota State Patrol is on the other end." Kimberley merged the call as she had been contacted because she was listed as her grandfather emergency contact.

As the reality of the situation unfolded, the trooper's voice emerged from the phone. The family was informed that Papa Joe had been attacked and was suffering from hypothermia and a severe head injury and is currently in an induced coma. The trooper continued to explain they were responding to a distress signal when Rose's frantic voice burst through, desperate and raw. "What about my daughter? She's pregnant!"

"Mrs. White, I regret to inform you that when we arrived, the home was engulfed in flames. Your father was fortunate to escape, but we cannot confirm who else was inside. The house has been completely destroyed, " the trooper explained.

In that moment, Rose and Kimberley crumbled under the weight of the devastating news. Tears streamed down Kimberley's face as guilt twisted in her gut. Overwhelmed by anxiety, she began to hyperventilate, gasping for air as panic seized her, feeling like everything was her fault. She felt responsible; she had brought

Christopher to Summer's front door. Sensing her distress, Justin quickly acted dialing 911. Kimberley had to be transported by EMS to the local hospital, where she could receive help.

"Additionally," the agent continued, "We've been contacted by the FBI and have been updated on the situation. Mrs. White, I'm sorry for everything your family is going through, but it's vital that you travel back to Minnesota. The FBI needs to speak with you, and your family."

Just then, they received an incoming call from an FBI agent stationed in Minnesota. The agent advised David that it would be inadvisable for either family member to travel independently. "An agent is en route to your location to escort your family back to Minnesota, just a few cities over, where you can catch a flight directly in," he advised.

David, however, steeled himself against the suggestion. "I'll be catching the next flight out to Washington to be by my daughter's side," he asserted firmly. "I will wait until Rose is safely picked up before leaving out." The thought of losing another child ignited a fierce resolve within him.

Rose sat next to him, her eyes vacant and lost, silently praying for Summer's safety, hoping against hope that her daughter had managed to escape the inferno yet was simply unable to reach out for help. Though her heart ached, she knew she must head to Minnesota to assist the FBI in their urgent search for Summer. At the same time, David and Kimberley would coordinate with agents tackling the distressing case of baby Asher's kidnapping in Washington, a dark irony that weighed heavily on them all.

CHAPTER: 28
I WANT JUSTICE

Rose was swiftly returned to Minnesota within hours. The gravity of the situation felt so frightening, and the urgency was palpable in every swift movement of the agents surrounding her; their purposeful strides hinted at the seriousness of the situation. As they walked, a heavy dread clung to her. They offered to escort her to the hospital where her father had been flown, but she declined with a firm shake of her head. Her heart raced at the thought of her daughter and grandson; they were her foremost priorities, and she had to focus on them.

Fear consumed her; her rock, David, was not by her side to comfort her. Over the years, whenever David had not been by her side, she had learned to lean on Stevin, and now he was gone. Rose was ushered into a small, stark room. The door closed behind her with a soft click. She could feel the tension in the air, particularly when one of the agents received a call. The grave expression on his face suggested they were grappling with crucial information, yet she remained in the dark, anxiety gnawing at her insides as she was left alone in the room.

A quiet but firm tap on the door jolted her from her racing thoughts. When the agents entered, one stood out, his head bowed and shoulders drooping, his body language screaming the weight of bad news.

Before they could utter a word, Rose shot up from her chair, fear gripping her heart. Panic surged through her like an electric shock as she cried out, "WHERE IS MY DAUGHTER?" Her voice echoed off the sterile walls, a desperate plea laced with anguish that reverberated in the stillness of the room.

I'm sorry to have to inform you, Mrs. White, but remains were discovered in a room at the front of the home. It appears that your daughter was inside when the fire started.

As the news sank in, Rose's legs buckled beneath her, and she collapsed to the floor in shock. Both agents rushed to her side, lifting her gently into a nearby chair. One agent darted out of the room, returning with a bottle of water.

Rose's body stiffened with disbelief as she suddenly stopped mid-scream and immediately pushed back against the idea that it could be Summer. "No, no! This can't be right," she protested, her voice quivering. "It's not my daughter. Christopher is behind this; he's done this before. He's a sick, twisted individual. He's taken her before, leaving us in agony, believing she was deceased. No, this isn't right. That's not my daughter," she wailed.

"We genuinely understand how difficult this is for you," one agent replied softly, his tone steady yet compassionate. "We are aware of the allegations surrounding Christopher. Summer's father-in-law provided our agents in Washington with a detailed file that Stevin apparently kept, chronicling the troubling incidents involving Christopher and his family. I must be candid: if any of these accusations are true, I have to ask, why didn't anyone involve the authorities sooner?"

Rose's voice was laced with pain and remorse as she responded, "We tried! We did everything we could! My daughter did everything she could! And we all failed her. So, please forgive me if I find all this a bit too convenient for Christopher. This could be his elaborate scheme to fake my daughter's death and whisk her off to who knows where. She's pregnant! I'm begging you, please help her!"

"Don't worry, Mrs. White, our forensic scientist will identify the remains; we just need to collect a DNA sample from you. We've arranged for you to stay in a comfortable hotel room nearby. After we collect the sample, we'll escort you there, and one of our female agents will accompany you for your safety."

Rose shook her head; desperation etched on her face. "No, please take me to my father," she requested. He was the one who held all the answers she desperately sought. He had to regain conscience.

CHAPTER: 29
CHRISTOPHER STRIKES AGAIN

The family's hopes for resolution seem to diminish daily as each passing day chipped away at their optimism. It had been three agonizing weeks, marked by desperate searching and unanswered questions, with no signs of Asher or Summer. David and Kimberley had returned to the haunting familiarity of Minnesota, where they remained by Rose's side, clinging to one another in their shared grief.

Daily, they took turns sitting at the hospital, surrounded by the sterile smells and dull sounds of machines, while their makeshift home, a cramped hotel room that seemed to echo their despair. In a single, devastating day, they lost four family members. With Summer's due date looming just two days away, the weight of their circumstances grew heavier.

David was suffocating under his grief, mourning Stevin, Summer, and the babies, and now, helplessly watching Rose struggling. It was as if he had lost her, too. She walked around like an empty shell, moving through each day like a shadow of her former self, rejecting any comfort that might ease her pain. With each passing day, the grim reality sank in more heavily upon them, indicating that the remains likely belonged to Summer. Yet Rose clung desperately to denial; she refused to allow her mind to even process that possibility. Her hatred for the Diamond family grew stronger with each passing day, seemingly fueling her determination to keep going.

The last update they had received was that Christopher was a potential suspect who was wanted for questioning but could not be located. His parents, having undergone multiple interviews, insisted that their son knew nothing of the situation and that it was not unusual for him to disappear for months being unreachable. Meanwhile, Mr. Diamond's lawyer expertly shielded his client, stifling any legal threats and shielding them from the relentless scrutiny of the FBI.

Rose and her family were summoned to a briefing with the attending physician and a patient advocate regarding her father's delicate condition. The waiting room was bustling with local family members, all of whom were grieving alongside Rose and Kimberley. While Rose did not have a strong connection to her father's side of the family, feeling distant and disconnected, Kimberley had grown quite close to them.

As the family gathered in the conference room, the doctor gravely informed them that it had been a week since Papa Joe was taken out of his induced coma, and he had not responded positively. Although the swelling in his brain was gradually decreasing, his progress remained slow. The doctor presented a heart-wrenching option to cease all medical interventions and simply observe how he would respond while simultaneously providing the family with hospice paperwork. A stark reminder of their grim reality.

In a surge of unbearable emotions, Rose snapped, slamming her hand on the table and yelling, "I can't, I just can't," before storming out the conference room, demanding that David take her home to Atlanta, leaving Kimberley and the cousins with the difficult decision of whether to end life support.

Though Papa Joe remained stable in his condition, he still had not regained consciousness, prompting a difficult decision to relocate him to a long-term facility closer to his family, with the hopes he would improve. Kimberley returned to Atlanta with her parents. Despite her love for her grandfather, she felt her parents needed her, and she was anxious and fearful of Christopher and his increasingly unpredictable, dangerous behavior.

Springfield Illinois

Ebony twirled joyfully around her spacious new home, the warmth of the golden rays spilling through the large windows and illuminating the freshly painted walls. She and Thomas had finally upgraded, expanding the square footage and purchasing their dream home; life was good. Although she missed her best friend, Summer, she was relieved to be free from the chaos that Christopher had brought into their lives, a shadow that threatened her family's peace. For years, ever since Summer had escaped his grasp, Christopher made it his mission to sink Thomas's successful business as a twisted form of revenge to punish Ebony. The strain had become unbearable, and Thomas ultimately had to sell his beloved company. In a daring leap, he and Ebony took a risky risk and went into business together, cutting all ties to Diamond's name and embracing a fresh start.

Despite everything, Ebony felt grateful knowing that Summer was happy with Stevin and living her best life. Her cousin Sophia had spotted Summer at the airport while traveling, and Summer had proudly shared how well she was doing and how she had found love. Unbeknownst to Summer, Sophia had secretly taken pictures of her and Stevin together at the airport and showed the photos to Ebony. She recognized Stevin in the photos and leaped for joy, knowing that everything had come full circle for Summer. Stevin had always been her pick for Summer, so she felt reassured that Summer was happy and well taken care of, as Stevin was always a gentleman.

Ebony was startled by the sound of her doorbell. She quickly snatched her tablet off the bed and checked the front door camera. A figure appeared, his back slightly turned to the camera, cradling a toddler on his hip. Assuming it was just a neighbor stopping by to welcome her to the neighborhood, she hurried down the stairs and flung open the door.

But the moment she laid eyes on him, a rush of shock coursed through her. She stumbled back, nearly dropping her tablet in disbelief. Christopher pushed right in without an invite. He was unrecognizable on the camera. He wore a worn baseball cap that shadowed his face; he had allowed his hair to grow out in a mini fro and sported unkempt facial hair. He looked very thin and had lost weight. His gaunt frame revealed the toll life had taken on him and the muscular physique he once had seemed to have withered away.

He strode into her home, plopping himself down on the sofa while bouncing the small toddler on his lap in a tender yet awkward gesture. The baby boy's eyes were swollen and red, and his bottom lip stuck out with big crocodile tears streaming down his flushed cheeks. As soon as Ebony saw the baby, she knew he belonged to Summer; he had Summer's kind eyes and resembled Stevin's features.

Keeping her composure, she asked, "What can I do for you, Christopher?"

"Where's Thomas?" he asked, scanning her home with a hardened gaze. "I see you guys have done well for yourselves."

"He's on his way home," she said, feeling her heart race, masking the sting of the realization that Thomas wasn't due back for several hours.

"Well, I'm looking for Summer." At the mention of his mother's name, Baby Asher's head popped up, looking around with tearful eyes before his crying intensified. It was evident that Christopher struggled to comfort him; he seemed to have no experience with children, let alone babies.

Ebony walked over to them, "Can I hold him," she asked, scooping Asher out of Christopher's arms before he could reply. Asher immediately wrapped his arms around Ebony's neck, laying his head on her shoulder before falling to sleep, his little body jerking as he sniffed from exhaustion.

"I need a drink. Where is your bar?" Christopher said, not pausing for an answer; he wandered through her home as if he were an invited guest. When he located a bottle of brandy, he poured himself a generous glass and downed it in one swift motion as if he were quenching an unbearable thirst.

"I'm here for his mom; she ran off."

"Christopher, I haven't seen or spoken with Summer since she disappeared from your home," she stated firmly, trying to maintain her composure.

"So you're telling me you didn't know about our son?" he shot back, searching her face for honesty.

"No, Christopher! Why would Summer run off and leave her son behind? His anger flared, and he marched toward her, snatching Asher out of her arms. The baby immediately erupted into tears, his little face crumpling in distress.

"Tell that bitch that the way to her son is through me," he seethed, storming out the door, leaving a whirlwind of emotions lingering in the air.

Ebony hurriedly locked the door, her fingers trembling as she slid the heavy metal bolts into place. Her heart raced as she dashed to the window, peering through the glass with wide, anxious eyes. She watched intently as Christopher's car pulled away. She scanned every detail of the vehicle he was driving.

The image of Summer cradling her child flickered in her thoughts. There was no way Summer would willingly leave her baby in Christopher's care. He would have had to pry her child away from her, and the mere thought of that sent a chill down Ebony's spine. Her heart ached at the possibility that Christopher had done something to harm Summer.

Ebony's heart raced faster as she quickly typed Summer's name into the search bar on her tablet, her fingertips trembling against the keys. As the search yielded no results, a sense of dread settled over her. Desperately, she typed Stevin's name, and her world seemed to shatter as the headline news article flashed across the screen. The chilling words detail Stevin's tragic death, violently taken from the world. As well as the harrowing kidnapping of his son, Asher Bash. Ebony's hands shook as she scrolled through the article, her mind racing to find a way to report Christopher, the man she feared. Ebony was directed to her local FBI field office, where she reported Asher's sighting with Christopher. She was directed to an agent,

Susan Bell; Ebony poured out every detail about Christopher's chilling visit and Asher's distressing condition.

"Agent Bell," she implored, her voice filled with desperation.

"Summer was my best friend. There's no way she would ever let Christopher take her child. The report didn't mention her at all; you have to issue a missing person report on her!"

Agent Bell's voice remained stoic. "Mrs. Holmes, have you had any contact with Summer's family?"

"No! Someone claiming to be her sister visited me a couple of years ago, but she left no contact information."

"Mrs. Holmes, when was the last time you spoke with Summer?"

"I haven't heard from Summer since she fled Illinois on the run from Christopher."

"Mrs. Holmes, I regret to inform you that Summer's home has been reported as having burned down in what is believed to be an act of arson. An unidentified body was discovered in the wreckage, and it is presumed to be Summer."

A profound silence enveloped Ebony, her mind reeling in disbelief. "Hello? Mrs. Holmes?" Agent Bell's voice echoed through the line, but all that filled the void was the haunting realization of what had just been said. No response came, only the quiet hum of the connection—like a gaping chasm where hope once resided.

CHAPTER: 30
WELCOME HOME

Rose picked up her phone as she stared at the unknown number flashing on the screen. With a huff of frustration, she set the phone back down on her unmade bed, where clothes were strewn carelessly. For days, she had been bombarded by relentless calls from the press and mysterious numbers, each one claiming to have information about Asher's whereabouts and eager to get their hands on the reward money.

Needing to escape the suffocating atmosphere and desperate for a breath of fresh air, she stepped outside and sank into one of the creaky wooden chairs on the front porch. Her gaze wandered to the street, rolling her eyes at the sight of a patrol unit cruising by the house. It felt as if she was imprisoned in her own home, each day dragging on like a drawn-out life sentence.

While she was grateful for agencies working tirelessly to secure her family's safety, a dark part of her secretly wished they would vanish and allow the big bad wolf, Christopher, to come and attempt to burn her house down. She inhaled deeply, trying to calm the storm of emotions swirling inside her, especially the seething rage she held towards Christopher and his family. Each breath was a battle against the rage that threatened to consume her. The tension clenched her chest, making it feel heavier with every thought.

Rose was startled as David car suddenly veered into the driveway, tires screeching to a halt. It seemed as though he had leaped from the car before he had fully come to a stop and put the car in park.

"Rose, what's going on? Why haven't you been answering your phone?"

Rose stared back, a look of confusion on her face, as he hurriedly walked towards her, waving his phone in his hand, seeking her attention.

"Go ahead, Agent, Kennedy. I have Rose right here!"

The agent, speaking in a low and serious tone, delivered news that sent shockwaves through Rose. Christopher had shown up at Ebony's home with Asher, claiming to be looking for Summer, alleging she had run off, abandoning the baby.

As the agent continued, he issued a stark warning: that the information was to remain confidential. Christopher's every move was now under surveillance. He was scheduled to land at a private hangar in Los Angeles, traveling aboard a client's private jet. The FBI had meticulously planned to follow him discreetly, uncovering the identities of those who were aiding him.

Los Angeles, The Diamonds Estate

"Nate, security just notified me that Christopher is on his way to the main house, and Nate, he has that child with him!"

"He has what?" Mr. Diamond's voice boomed with alarm, practically leaping out of his plush leather reading chair. The newspaper crumpled beneath his grip as it fell to the floor. His glasses nearly slipped off his face as panic flashed in his eyes. "Tell them to stop him right now! Don't allow him access into the main house!"

Agitated, he lunged for the intercom phone on the mahogany side table, his heart racing as he barked orders to the security team, demanding they intercept Christopher and escort him off the property. Turning sharply to his wife, a storm of frustration brewing in his chest, he spat, "That reckless son of yours is going to drag us all down into his mess."

Before he could unleash another furious command, Christopher walked in through the main door, cradling an exhausted Asher in his arms. Mrs. Diamond rushed forward, desperation on her face as she reached out to take her grandson from Christopher. But Asher, sensing the tension and confusion, let out a wail that pierced the air, clinging tightly to the very stranger who had abducted him.

"Son," his mother said, her hand gently brushing against his face. "You don't look well, son," noticing his disheveled appearance and significant weight loss.

"Are you completely out of your mind? Why on earth would you bring that child here, of all places? Did you kill his mother?" Mr. Diamond's voice dripped with disdain, his expression contorting in disgust as he glared at Christopher. "No, don't you dare answer that!" he shouted, a vein pulsing in his temple. "I won't be dragged into your insanity again! You're acting with a level of irresponsibility that threatens everything. You're reckless and have no respect for what I've built for my family, not your family, not your empire, but mine!" His anger erupted in a furious display as he swept his arms wide, sending picture frames crashing to the floor.

"Honey, get Bob on the line, right now!" he commanded. He'll need legal counsel immediately. You'd better be a damn good liar, because if not, you better master it quickly. You will have Bob contact the authorities and report someone contacted you demanding a million-dollar ransom for your son."

Before Mr. Diamond could finish his sentence, the front door exploded open as federal agents stormed in, ordering everyone to the ground. In a flurry of uniforms and authority, Baby Asher was swiftly snatched away from Christopher's grasp and taken out of the home to safety. Moments later, Rose and David received the call that Asher had been found and was safe, a glimmer of hope in a darkening storm.

Atlanta Georgia, Welcome Home Asher

The entire family was restless; their anticipation of Asher's arrival had everyone on edge. While David and Kimberley succumbed to exhaustion, Rose remained by the window, eagerly awaiting the arrival of her grandson. Her tired eyes were heavy and red from sleeplessness, and she stifled a yawn as the old wall clock ticked away, signaling the arrival of 6 AM.

Kimberley entered the living room; her voice laced with concern as she asked her mother if she had managed to catch even a moment of sleep. Just as Rose was about to respond, she spotted a black sedan pulling up the driveway. A surge of energy surged through her, and she bolted out the door, leaving Kimberley hurriedly racing to awaken David.

As Rose rushed toward the car, she came to a halt at the back door, her heart swelling as she paused and took in the sight of her beautiful grandson inside. Tears streamed down her cheeks as she soaked in the sight of him; he was a perfect reflection of his parents. Though she felt she had failed Summer, she was determined not to fail Asher. When baby Asher recognized her, he tossed his sippy cup onto the floorboard and pressed his tiny hand against the cool glass. It was a moment of pure connection. In that instant, she couldn't unbuckle him fast enough as he wriggled and squirmed, desperate to free himself from the restraints of his car seat.

Finally cradling him in her arms, Rose felt an overwhelming rush of love wash over her as he laid his head on her shoulder, playfully tugging at her ear. She walked back into the house; Asher held tightly in her arms while David and Kimberley waited patiently for their turn to embrace him. Asher glanced around, unsure of how to react, reaching first for Kimberley, then for his Pop-Pop, before returning once again to the comfort of his grandmother's warm embrace.

He slept for days so soundly that Rose often had to gently rouse him to eat. Concern gnawed at her heart as she pondered what he might have witnessed and the haunting memories he might carry. While uncertainty surrounded Summer's fate, one thing was clear: Asher was with Stevin during his final moments. Although he is just a toddler, Rose couldn't help but wonder if he could remember the horrible events Christopher had exposed him to.

CHAPTER: 31
SEEKING JUSTICE

Atlanta Georgia

Kimberley sat quietly in the dimly lit family room, her thoughts racing with unspoken worries. She watched as Rose devoted all her attention entirely to baby Asher. He seemed to be the only thing that had brought their family a little sunlight in their dark storm. Suddenly, the doorbell chimed, alerting her that someone was detected at the door. She wasn't anxious or afraid; between the sign-in guard at the gate, her honorary uncles close, and the constant patrolling of their home, she knew the visitor was likely someone visiting in an official capacity. Nevertheless, she proceeded with caution, checking the security monitor before she answered the door.

To her surprise, it was Detective Shaw. Hesitating to answer the door, she dreaded having to face his "I told you so" stare. She already felt burdened by guilt for this entire situation. After calling out for her dad numerous times without a response, she had no choice but to face him.

With a deep inhale that steadied her nerves, she swung open the door, "Hello, Detective. Come in; let me get my parents." To her surprise, he embraced her with a hug and asked how she was holding up. Just then, David and Rose entered the room, drawn by the doorbell. Asher clung tightly to his grandmother's shirt.

Rose stepped forward to embrace him with a light hug and a pat on the back after David had given him a firm handshake.

"Has something happened, Detective Shaw?" Rose asked, feeling confused about his visit, especially since everything that had recently occurred was completely out of his jurisdiction.

"I don't know if you guys are aware, but Christopher was arraigned today." He hesitated, a flicker of anger crossing his features. "He didn't enter a plea; instead, his father and his paid corrupt associates had him placed in a psychiatric hospital."

David's expression twisted into a mask of fury as he clenched his fists, "And let me guess, they're pushing for a Not Guilty by Reason of Insanity plea?"

"Not exactly," Detective Shaw replied, shaking his head. "I suspect he'll plead not guilty. They're stalling for time because he's deemed a flight risk. His attorney anticipated that the judge would have likely denied his bail. And as we know, his father's pockets reach deep; they're probably ensuring he's in a lavish suite in the psychiatric unit rather than a typical facility. The attorney is arguing that Christopher is a high-profile inmate who requires a separate housing unit and a specific medical facility."

Leaning closer, Detective Shaw lowered his voice to a conspiratorial whisper, "But I'm not here in an official compacity; I'm here as a friend, off the record. The Diamond family's version of events is this: Christopher received an anonymous call supposedly on the day of Stevin's murder. An unknown voice claimed that his son, Asher, had been kidnapped and demanded a ransom for his safety and release. According to Christopher, during the exchange, he was blindfolded and held captive for an agonizing week. After what felt like an eternity of uncertainty, he was finally released and reunited with his son since being taken from the hospital by Summer.

Christopher claims the kidnappers held him to ensure the authorities weren't contacted per their agreement. Once freed, he believed it was Summer, being influenced by Stevin, who wanted money to run off together and didn't want to be burdened with another man's child. Claiming that's why he visited Ebony, searching for Summer, hoping to uncover the truth as to why she would abandon their son. He denies any knowledge of Stevin's death until told by the FBI."

"Kimberley, unable to contain her outrage, burst out, "That sick weirdo knows my nephew isn't his son! His entire story is complete bullshit." Her voice echoed with disbelief and anger, punctuating the tension in the room.

David walked over to Kimberley to comfort her, noticing how visibly shaken she had become. Her hands trembled, with her fingers fidgeting in an anxious rhythm.

Detective Shaw continued, "The reason for my visit is to ensure you guys have all the resources you need to nail this 'son of a bitch.' I was called in for a meeting with internal affairs, who have reopened the case surrounding Summer's kidnapping. Strangely, my investigation is now under intense scrutiny. They are examining every aspect of the case under a magnifying glass, with criticism directed at my failure to pursue the trail of Stevin and Summer's financial dealings. Ironically, the TSA officer has suddenly retracted her original statement. Her revised account suggests that perhaps Summer wasn't kidnapped, and she may have been willing to leave the country on her own accord. This scenario has the Diamond's name written all over it.

"One thing that works in our favor is that the bodyguard, Brody's sister-in-law, came forward with her sister's diary. Apparently, she had been journaling her fears and events that started occurring to her and her husband after Summer escaped from the hospital. Some of her entries even admit that she was aware Summer was being held against her will while staying at the Diamond's estate. Their car accident is now being reopened to determine if it was accidental or criminal. From what I heard, the diary contains detailed incidents indicating her and Brody's lives were in danger."

Rose sat quietly throughout the entire meeting with Detective Shaw, her posture straight but tense as he spoke. Not a single word escaped her lips; she was like a statue, her expression as blank as the pale walls around her. The only movement was the occasional flicker of her eyes, which appeared distant and unfocused as if she were miles away. Rose's mind seemed to drift to a different world, a world where her only concern was the soft cooing of Asher and his safety.

Finally, in a gentle but deliberate motion, she rose from her chair and walked over to the playpen in the corner. Asher, with his bright, wide eyes, reached out for her. Rose, with a protective instinct that seemed to radiate from her, scooped him up, his tiny frame fitting snugly against her chest. With Asher securely in her arms, she paused for a moment, glancing back at Detective Shaw before turning and exiting the room.

Rose watched from the upstairs bedroom window as David walked the detective to his car to see him off. Sitting on the edge of the bed, she gently cradled Asher, rocking him in her arms as he peacefully drifted off to sleep. As she looked down at him, his tiny eyes fluttering in his sleep. She could only imagine what his little mind could remember.

Closing her eyes softly, a wave of nostalgia washed over her, filled with the sweet memories of the joy that Summer had brought to her and James. In that quiet moment, she realized with a heavy heart that she would have to make an unimaginable sacrifice to protect her grandson.

CHAPTER: 32
THE UNTHINKABLE SACRIFICE

David gradually blanked the sleep from his eyes as the bright sunlight poured through the window. Missing from his usual morning view was Rose, changing Asher at the changing table; as half of their bedroom had been transformed into Asher's nursery. He stretched his arm back, reaching for Rose, thinking that perhaps she had decided to sleep in while Kimberley took care of the baby. But her side of the bed felt cold to touch, and Asher's crib was empty.

A growing sense of worry crept in as he made his way downstairs, wandering from room to room in search of Rose; each room he entered was cold and empty of their presence. When he entered the kitchen, he noticed a letter from Rose propped up against the coffee pot. He unfolded the letter, but after only a few seconds of reading, it slipped from his fingers and floated to the floor as he sank into a chair at the table.

Kimberley shuffled into the kitchen with a big yawn and stretched, asking the whereabouts of Rose and Asher. She was so focused on stuffing her mouth with the leftover banana bread that she didn't notice the tears forming in her father's eyes. When the silence lingered, and he didn't reply, she glanced up at him and saw him silently pointing to the note lying beneath her fuzzy pink house shoes. She picked the letter up and began to read the three lines that didn't explain much: "Don't worry about me and Asher. I have made an executive decision to return Asher to the Bash family for his safety and to ensure he has the nurturing environment he deserves while I focus on justice for his parents. I will return in three days!"

As her last words sank in, the silence between them was heavy with unspoken thoughts, leaving both of them to grapple with the looming uncertainty that now shadowed their lives.

Mr. Bash slowly rose from his weathered rocking chair, its familiar creak a painful reminder of the passage of time filled with memories of his boys. He looked out towards his dirt driveway, where a cloud of dust swirled, signaling the arrival of an unexpected visitor. Since Stevin's funeral service, guests had been few from far, and the house was filled with an unusually heavy silence. Mrs. Irene's grief was unbearable, and the family had chosen to keep their distance, allowing her time to mourn, unsure of how to comfort her in her sorrow. It was painfully clear that joy had been uprooted; the once vibrant, family-oriented, and warm-hearted woman she had been had faded. The comforting aroma of daily home-cooked meals, filled with spices and love, no longer exists. A clear sign that joy had been stripped away as she grieved her son's tragic death.

Mr. Bash clutched the porch railing, his fingers tracing the familiar grooves as he carefully made his way down, step by step. Grief had taken a toll on him physically, making him appear as though he had aged a full decade. He instantly recognized Rose when she stepped out of the car and walked around to the back passenger door. He caught a glimpse of Asher, his little head bobbing with excitement as Rose unbuckled him from his safety seat.

Suddenly, a surge of energy coursed through him; his tired, aching knees seemed to regain strength as he started running towards Rose and his grandson. Without hesitation, Rose rushed into his arms and embraced him with a hug. The mere fact that he could relate to her grief and understood her pain helped him break through the shield of grief she had built around herself. As she let out a gut-wrenching cry, he hugged her tighter. Mr. Bash didn't hold back and allowed his own tears to flow freely, embracing vulnerability in that moment and breaking through the isolating silence of their pain. They stood together, two grieving parents united in their unimaginable loss, finding solace in their shared sorrow.

Rose's heartrending cry was muffled out by Mrs. Irene's high-pitched scream when she caught sight of her grandson. Although Rose had once despised the very ground, Mrs. Irene walked on because of her cruel treatment of Summer; at that moment, all bitter feelings were cast aside. After all, she was a grieving mother also; Rose knew the lifeline that baby Asher brought back into her life, and if she could mend just a tiny piece of their shattered heart, she was willing to try.

Mrs. Irene stood frozen, tears streaming down her cheeks at the sight of her grandson. With gentle determination, Rose approached her, placing Asher in her trembling arms. She stood shoulder to shoulder with Mrs. Irene, softly rubbing Asher's back, offering comfort in the storm of emotions. Mrs. Irene tightly gripped Rose's hand, holding on to both her and Asher. They shared a silent moment where words felt unnecessary; a deep-seated pain bound them both, their shared grief a heavy burden that they both carried. They knew that neither of their children deserved the cruel fate that had befallen them. Now, they had a shared mutual interest that required them all to band together.

Asher nestled in his grandmother's arms, his tiny head turning from side to side as he looked over everyone's shoulder, searching for his dad. Impatiently, he kicked and squirmed to be put down, running to the door with his tiny little fist bald knocking on the screen door. Mr. Bash opened the door, and Asher seized hold of his finger, leading him toward the back of the house in the direction of his father's room. The sight tugged painfully at Mrs. Irene's heart as she watched her innocent grandson march purposefully toward his father's room in search of him. Confirming his little memories were filled with the happier days they shared when visiting the farm. Rose instinctively stepped back onto the porch, unable to endure the haunting cries that escaped Mrs. Irene.

Mrs. Irene scooped Asher up and held him in close, wrapping her arms around him protectively while clutching a cherished picture of Stevin. The silent ache in her heart was palpable as Asher continued to call out for his "Dada."

Moments later, Mr. Bash returned to the porch with Rose; the collective sadness between them all was too much to bear. Rose made her way back to the car, returning with two large duffle bags. "I need you both to take care of my grandson, and I will pursue justice for our kids. My husband informed me that when you visited last, you and Stevin shared a wealth of information regarding the Diamonds during your men's night out. I implore you; whatever you have on this demonic family, please pass it along to the FBI. This is our moment to seek justice, and I intend to do just that," she said as she said her goodbyes and walked away without hugging Asher goodbye. She needed to remain focused, knowing that if she had another choice, she could never willingly say goodbye to him.

CHAPTER: 33
PREPARING FOR WAR!

Rose returned home, her face a mask of silence, offering no explanation for her abrupt solo decision to relocate Asher back to Washington. Anxiety gnawed at David; here he was, a licensed psychiatrist, yet he felt utterly powerless that he couldn't provide the emotional support his wife so desperately needed. With Asher's joyful presence now absent from their home and no longer bringing light into Rose's dark world, she had turned into a silent shadow. The dining area had become her office, cluttered with legal papers and documents scattered from wall to wall, as she spent endless hours preparing for court as if she were the prosecutor, prosecuting Christopher and his family.

David and Kimberley kept a watchful eye on Rose while giving her distance. Her inner turmoil hidden behind a facade of silence, leaving them with no insight into her true feelings.

As expected, Christopher's trial was expedited. The courtroom buzzed with an ironic tension. What should have been credible witnesses for the prosecution became scapegoats under the harsh scrutiny of the Diamond's sharp-tongued attorneys during cross-examination. Detective Shaw found himself under intense scrutiny on the stand, where he was mercilessly ripped apart. His close bond with the family was now a liability, and crucial legal protocols had been overlooked to safeguard Stevin's interest. The defense attorney seized upon these missteps, using them to Christopher's advantage.

Meanwhile, the shadow of doubt loomed large over the proceedings. Christopher had been committed during Summer's hospital stay, and due to her absence in court, the alleged kidnapping by him was only hearsay. This casting even more uncertainty over the trial.

Although the details surrounding Christopher's whereabouts remained uncertain, and the investigation was ongoing, there was a lack of evidence linking him to either crime scene. He was neither seen nor identified during the events surrounding Stevin's murder, the violent assault on Poppa Joe, or the arson of the family home. The haunting possibility of Summer's fate also lingers, as her body has yet to be identified in the smoldering ruins of the fierce fire. The lack of evidence presented the prosecution with significant challenges, as they were unable to conclusively place Christopher at either crime scene, leaving unanswered questions hanging in the air.

Stephanie and Dr. Brown's testimonies only served to incriminate Mr. Diamond. During cross-examination, the Diamond's attorney probed them both with pointed questions, pressing them on why, if they ever sensed or were informed that Summer was being held against her will, no official police report was ever filed. The attorney also inquired whether their documentation included any references to those serious concerns.

"Well, aren't you supposed to be mandated reporters, bound by law to report any suspected abuse?" the attorney inquired, a smug smile curling at the corners of his lips as Christopher leaned back in his chair, radiating confidence that filled the room.

Meanwhile, Ebony's testimony only added layers of complexity to the case. Confirming that Christopher had shown up at her home in search of Summer, which corroborates his claim that he had been kidnapped and held for the ransom of the child, only visiting Summer's best friend because he believed that Summer was behind the ransom demand. In their dramatic closing remarks, Christopher's attorney emphasized that Asher was not a Diamond, portraying Summer as a young woman who was promiscuous, carefree, and prone to disappearing on her own accord, which evoked a sense of recklessness about her character.

"We have heard multiple testimonies about Christopher's character. So, who is he? Is he the loving guy who cared for the less fortunate, giving her the life that she could only dream of? Her passport shows he flew her around the world. Or is he a brutal woman-beater?

"Yet, there is not a single police report or any medical records from Illinois documenting this horrific abuse. Not one friend, not one family member ever reported any of the claims made during this trial. You even heard the startling testimony from her own sister. She confessed to carrying on a secret love affair with her sister's boyfriend behind her back, betraying her trust. Kimberley also admitted to seeing Summer the night of the alleged kidnapping. When interviewed by Detective Shaw, Kimberley stated, "She didn't look like she was in distress. She didn't ask for help." In fact, Kimberely felt so at ease with Christopher and Summer's interaction that she waited an entire day before telling her parents of Summer's whereabouts. Some may question: Is this relentless pursuit of Christopher really justice, or is it Kimberley's own act of revenge?

Hey, if I'm Summer, I'd wonder why I even need friends and family like this; I would run off to!"

With a surge of anger, Rose bolted out of the courtroom doors, her chest heavy as she panted to catch her breath. David rushed behind her, and she fell into his arms, "David, they're painting her out to be the monster while labeling us all as liars. What kind of justice system allows this? How can this be the justice system we believe in? Take me home, please take me home!"

As they made their way out of the courthouse, the atmosphere shifted slightly. Surrounding them were the sheriff's deputies, who had grown fond of their family and empathized with their situation. Their expressions softened with genuine concern as they hugged Rose and spoke encouraging words. Each gesture reminded Rose that, amidst the chaos, there were those who stood by her.

Today was a significant day; it was the day of the verdict. Rose left the house bright and early without a word, so Kimberley and David decided to take her car, assuming Rose had chosen to drive herself. Rose returned home thirty minutes before court was due to start, pulling into the driveway and gesturing for David to open her car door. When he swung open the back door, to their surprise, which turned to confusion when they noticed a wheelchair in the backseat.

"David, can you please lift this into the back of your truck? And Kimberley, I think it's best if you sit this one out today," Rose said.

Kimberley's expression twisted with shock and anger. She felt a surge of betrayal rise within her. With a frustrated huff, she refused her mother's request, jamming the keys into her ignition and speeding away, her tires screeching against the pavement.

"Rose, why on earth do you have this wheelchair?"

"Well, maybe if I show up in a wheelchair, I'll get a little sympathy; God knows the truth hasn't mattered much," Rose replied, a hint of bitterness lacing her words."

"Why, Rose, of all days, would you choose to pick a fight with Kimberley? You can't overlook her feelings or the heavy burden this entire situation has placed on everyone. Why alienate her on such an important day?" David pressed.

"David, sometimes I need Kimberley to listen to me; it's for her own good!" She said, mumbling under her breath.

The car ride was silent; Rose stared out the truck window, her eyes wide open as she barely registered her surroundings. She was lost in thoughts that raced too fast for her to grasp. David sat tense, a silent prayer forming on his lips, desperately hoping that justice was on their side today, knowing Rose couldn't handle another crushing blow. The fear of losing her loomed over him.

As David parallel parked, he noticed Kimberley entering the courthouse alone.

"David, I really wish you would back me up on this. Kimberley doesn't need to be here, today."

"Rose!" he responded.

"Don't worry about it, David, just get my wheelchair," she insisted.

"Rose, are you really going to make me push you in this ridiculous chair?"

"David, Please!" she urged, her eyes pleading with him to understand.

With a reluctant sigh, he complied, watching as Rose transferred into the wheelchair, clutching her small purse tightly under her arm. He felt even more confused as they entered the building. Suddenly, Rose swung her legs down, abruptly halting the wheelchair, her voice rising in a frantic cry. "I can't do this! I just can't! It's my daughter, my daughter, dammit!"

Within seconds, one of the usual deputies rushed to her side, pushing the wheelchair through the metal detector and whisking Rose away to a quiet side room. David stayed with her, his heart aching as he worked to calm her racing thoughts. Finally calmed, they entered the courtroom.

David sat next to Kimberley, who was wide-eyed, her body rigid and trembling as her gaze was locked straight ahead. The very sight of Christopher sent a jolt of terror through her; his smug demeanor and cold eyes sent a wave of fear crashing over her, leaving her paralyzed in her seat as tears streamed down her cheeks. David immediately understood Rose's request, not considering the impact Christopher's presence would have on Kimberley; she, too, was a victim of his sick manipulation.

Just a seat away, Rose was unable to offer any support as she sat, engulfed in a thick fog of confusion. The courtroom felt surreal to her as if everyone were moving in slow motion. The voices of the attorneys and the murmurs of the audience echoed like muffled whispers, distorted and distant as if she were underwater, unable to grasp the gravity of the moment.

The judge's voice cut through the atmosphere, requesting Christopher to rise as Jury Number Five prepared to announce their verdict. One by one, the jury's findings echoed through the courtroom like a death knell: not guilty on all counts. It struck the family like a physical blow. Kimberley and David's emotions erupted in a chorus of disbelief, and Kimberley's anguished scream of "NO!" pierced through the courtroom. The judge banged his gavel, demanding order in the courtroom.

The FBI held back, awaiting the judge's final pronouncement, as tension rippled throughout the courtroom. They hadn't anticipated this outcome; they were hoping they would be arresting the father-son duo and delivering justice to both Rose and Stevin's families. As soon as the last words fell from the judge's lips, agents flooded in and took Mr. Diamond into custody on the spot. As the agent carefully read Mr. Nate Diamond his Miranda rights, an unsettling feeling of vulnerability seized him.

It was then that he comprehended the gravity of his situation: he was facing serious charges of kidnapping and false imprisonment of Summer Teller. To make matters worse, he was finally implicated in the horrific second-degree murder of his two best friends, Johnny Clarke and Sammy Olie, a case that had haunted his childhood community since 1950.

Christopher and his mother loudly protested, their voices rising in a desperate plea for their attorneys to act quickly and do something. Meanwhile, on the other side of the courtroom, Rose remained in a fog of confusion and disbelief. The reality of the circumstances struck her: Christopher had won again. It felt as if the ground had vanished beneath her feet. Once again, Christopher had emerged unscathed, victorious in his cruel game. The triumphant smirk that stretched across his face after the verdict was read felt like a dagger to her heart. His cold, calculating eyes locked onto hers with a chilling intensity. He grinned, satisfied, casting a disdainful glance toward her and her family, reveling in the chaos he had sown.

As Mr. Diamond was being led away, the chaotic shuffle of the family members positioned Christopher beside the prosecution table; his back turned to Rose. She rose from her seat with an eerie deliberate slowness, her small purse slipping from her fingers onto the floor. In her hand, a .22 caliber handgun glinted, catching the light for a fleeting moment. Time seemed to freeze for Rose as the sound of gasping breaths around her became muffled, replaced by ringing in her ears. As the realization dawned on everyone in the courtroom, they instinctively dropped to the ground, seeking shelter from the chaotic scene.

Rose settled back into her seat; her gaze fixed on Christopher. He turned to her, disbelief etched across his face, his hand clutching the back of his head as he staggered before sinking to his knees directly in front of her.

Before David could react and reach Rose, the sheriff's deputies surged toward her, quickly piling on top of her and swiftly arresting her.

Mr. Diamond fought against the restraints of his handcuffs, desperation fueling his struggle to reach his son's side, but he was forcefully dragged from the courtroom, a helpless look of anguish on his face.

Meanwhile, Mrs. Diamond collapsed onto Christopher, her cries piercing the somber air as she screamed his name, a heart-wrenching sound that echoed off the courtroom walls. David and Kimberley sat frozen in shock as the surreal scene unfolded before them. As Rose was escorted out, her face remained an unsettling mask of blankness, devoid of any emotion, as if she were a spectator in her own tragic drama.

***

Rose had been detained for two long, harrowing months, refusing any contact with her family and declining to speak with the lawyer David had attained on her behalf. The weight of her isolation pressed down on everyone, but finally, a breakthrough occurred. The family was able to reach her, thanks to the gentle persistence of her psychiatrist, who encouraged a visit from her husband.

David sat in the small visitation booth, anxiety knotting his stomach as he stared nervously at the glass window that separated him from Rose. The phone mounted on the wall felt heavy in his trembling hand as he waited, each second stretching into what felt like an eternity. When the heavy door creaked open, his breath hitched at the sight of Rose. A female guard escorted her in, holding her elbow for support as she shuffled forward, her posture defeated.

David's heart sank as he watched her; she sat hunched over, her long, unkept hair cascading down to shield her face, refusing to make eye contact. The guards, understanding her circumstances, had developed a soft spot for her. One of the female guards gently took the phone from its cradle and offered it to Rose with a sympathetic smile.

With a heavy sigh, Rose finally gripped the receiver, her fingers brushing the cold plastic as if it were an anchor pulling her back to reality. Yet, she kept her head bowed with her eyes fixed on the floor, unyielding to the world around her.

"Baby, please look at me," David pleaded, his voice choked with emotion. "Rose, you have to fight. Kimberley and Asher need you to keep fighting for all of us."

After a long, agonizing pause, she finally raised her head. Her eyes were hollow, framed by dark circles that spoke of sleepless nights and unending worry. "David, take care of yourself. You can't afford to worry about me," she murmured, her voice barely above a whisper, laced with exhaustion.

"Rose, please listen to me," David urged, his voice steadier and more defiant as he fought to inject hope into their conversation. "Kimberley has started a FundMyGoal page in your name, and I haven't spent a single cent on your attorney fees; donations are pouring in daily, enough to keep you defended. I know you haven't read my letters, but I need you to hear this: Mr. Diamond and his wife have been convicted. The Bash family has worked side by side with me and Kimberley to help you. You must fight! Summer needs you to fight harder than ever. The remains discovered in the home were not hers — they weren't even human! Summer is alive, Rose! She and baby Zoey need you. We can find them together if you just hold on!"

As David's passionate plea sank into Rose's heart, a flicker of hope ignited within her. Color gradually returned to her cheeks, her features awakening from the shadows that had plagued her. With a sudden surge of determination, she shot up from her chair, her voice echoing off the stark white walls as she shouted, "GUARD!"

THE END!

The Author

Other Books By Shantanel Payne
Her Lost Words; Her Broken Silence
Finding Her Voice

www.ingramcontent.com/pod-product-compliance
Lightning Source LLC
Chambersburg PA
CBHW021010180626
46814CB00003B/1235